The Proposal Solution

The Boozy Book Club Series

By

Rose Bak

Table of Contents

Copyright

Cover by Paper or Pixels[1]

---

1.   https://paperorpixels.com/

About This Book

She needs a husband. He needs money for his mother's medical treatments. What could go wrong?

Liz

Baseball was in my blood. I'd grown up in the Seagulls stadium, learning all the ins and outs of running a minor league franchise. As the Chief Administrative Officer, everyone assumed that I'd take over for my father when he retires.

Everyone except my mother. She convinces my father and the investors that as a single, forty-five year old woman, I didn't have the maturity to run this team. With the fate of my beloved Seagulls at risk, I panic and do the one thing I never do: lie.

Henry

When my mom's job eliminates her position right when she's in the middle of cancer treatments, I need to make a lot of money—fast. My buddy suggests becoming a paid escort and I decide to give it a try. My first assignment is a big one: pose as some rich woman's fiancé. Should be a piece of cake, right?

Until I see my client and realize that I've got another big problem: I'm in love with my fake fiancé.

Liz is worried about our ten-year age gap and the fact that she's paying me to spend time with her. But all I'm worried about is how to turn this fake engagement into a real marriage because she might be baseball royalty, but I'm playing for keeps.

"The Proposal Solution" is a midlife, opposites attract, instalove romance with baseball, nosy friends, a sweet younger man, and a woman who can't cook dinner without starting a fire. Expect a fast and steamy story with a sweet happily ever after.

This book is part of the *"Boozy Book Club"* series. Each book in the series is a steamy standalone featuring a couple in their fifties, a nosy group of book club friends, matchmaking family members, and a sweet happily ever after that proves anyone can find love later in life.

Author's Note: This book was previously published as "The Marriage Solution" by Rose Bak

Join My Mailing List

Join Rose Bak's mailing list at bit.ly/RoseBakNewsletter[2]. You'll get a free book and be the first to hear about all the latest releases, special sales, free books, and funny stories about my dog.

Dedication

This book is dedicated to every woman who has blazed her way into a non-traditional career and dealt with a lot of bullshit along the way.

Liz

"Elizabeth!"

I closed my eyes and took a deep breath as I heard my mother's voice behind me. With my hand on the exit door, I thought I'd finally escaped this boring ass correspondent club dinner. Those press people really loved to talk about themselves when they got the chance.

Silently I chastised myself for not leaving with Nolan and Agnes. They wouldn't have noticed if I'd followed them. They were in that 'I want to rip your clothes off' stage of the relationship. Or they would be by the end of the night, if the steamy looks they'd been sending each other over dinner were anything to go by. I was happy for my new friend. Nolan was a great guy.

I turned around slowly, and my mother's eyes immediately went to my not so flat belly, her gaze pointed. At forty-five years old, you'd think I was immune to her subtle digs about my body, but sometimes they slid right past my defenses.

My mother had been a model in her youth. Even at seventy years old she was stunningly beautiful, slim and often mistaken for someone twenty years younger. She was the kind of woman who could live on lettuce and air for days at a time and was always completely put together.

Unfortunately for me, I took after my father's side of the family. The McNallys were all farmers and sheep herders before the famines brought them to America. We were short, a little bit stout, and we held onto our calories as protection against the next famine.

"What do you need, Mother?"

"Your father has been making noises about retiring next year," she said. "I just want you to know I'm not going to vote for you to replace him. I think the Seagulls need a different leader, one who's more...appropriate for the job."

It was all I could do not to physically recoil. I'd spent my life being a disappointment to my mother. I was too short, too curvy, my hair was too wild and, worst of all, I was too much of a tomboy. I'd spent my entire life following my father around the Seagulls stadium, living and breathing baseball.

"You know I have the same number of shares as your father does," she reminded me. "I'll block the vote to name you as successor."

Mom came from money and had also made a fortune during her modeling days. Somewhere along the line she'd invested some of her family's money to buy shares in the team when it was struggling financially. Between her and my father they owned eighty percent of the team. Mom withholding her forty percent vote would make it difficult for me to take over the club, even with my father's support.

I made no effort to conceal my irritation at my mother's latest insult.

"What is this really about, Mother? You know as well as I do that I've given my heart and soul, my whole life, to this baseball team. I made it to Chief Administrative Officer on my own merit, through my own hard work, and I know the ins and outs of the business as much as Dad does at this point. So please, tell me why tonight of all nights you've decided to betray me and shit on my lifelong dream?"

My mother just blinked at me for a few long seconds. I rarely stood up to her like this – preferring to mostly ignore her until she moved onto something else—but the Seagulls were too important not to fight for.

"It was Nolan and Agnes," she finally admitted. "Seeing them together, so much in love, it reminded me of how it was when I met your father. I want that for you, Elizabeth. It's too late for you to have children, but you should at least have a companion. Someone to love you in your old age."

"I thought my parents loved me," I said bitterly. "Maybe that's only true for one of them."

Mom reeled back like I'd slapped her.

"If you really cared for me, you'd want to support the thing that makes me happiest – my career. You know good and well that I've never been interested in getting married because I'm married to my job."

"I'll support your career Liz, when you can show me that you're serious about a relationship with something besides a baseball team. You need a husband to take care of you."

My mouth dropped. "Are you trying to blackmail me into getting married?"

"If that's what it takes," Mother sniffed haughtily.

I stepped closer, getting into her space. She was five inches taller than me, so when I spoke, it was into her impressive cleavage. I knew for a fact that it was surgically enhanced, although she liked to pretend otherwise.

"You and I are done, Mother. You've gone too far this time."

My mother straightened up a little bit more. "Someday you'll thank me for this, Liz."

I took a step back and gave her my best glare. "Someday I'll be in charge of the Seagulls, and I'll wear my favorite jersey to dance on your grave."

Henry

"Hey buddy, how are you doing?"

I looked up as my best friend Gavin clasped my shoulder. Before I could respond, our friend Isaac joined us. The three of us tried to meet at least once or twice a month to catch up. We'd been friends since freshman year of high school and now, more than twenty years later, we were still tight.

It probably helped that none of us was married or in a serious relationship. The few times one of us had gotten serious about someone, it had inevitably messed up our guy time. Either the woman would want to join us, or she'd feel insecure about us hanging out at a bar having a drink, as if the only reason we were there was to pick up women. Or, in one memorable case when Gavin dated a self-professed Wiccan, the girlfriend would need male energy at a New Moon ceremony.

We ordered a pitcher of beer and a platter of wings as we started talking about football, cars, our jobs, and then our personal lives, in that order.

"I got some bad news," I told them as the platter of hot wings arrived.

"Is it your mom?" Isaac asked in concern. "I thought she was responding well to her treatments."

I nodded. "She is, better than they expected actually."

My mother was diagnosed with breast cancer about six months ago. It was a pretty aggressive case, but she'd been responding well to treatment and was currently on the list for a clinical trial that the doctor thought she'd be a perfect candidate for – if I could figure out how to keep her on his service.

"Her company laid her off. It's supposedly budget cuts, but Mom said they're self-insured for medical insurance so she's pretty sure they chose her because all of her medical bills are costing them too much money."

Both of my friends looked at me in shock.

"I thought it was illegal to fire someone with a medical condition," Gavin said.

I nodded. "It is. We talked to an attorney. The problem is that they fired a couple of people, including her, and blamed it on their budget so there's no way to prove it was directly related to her illness."

"Jesus Christ. What is she going to do?"

"I can't get her on Medicaid unless she sells her house, which she definitely doesn't want to do. Our only option is to buy private health insurance through the state exchange, but getting anything other than basic coverage is super expensive."

"How expensive?"

"Like five grand a month. And it's not like she can get a new job while she's sick. I'm trying to figure out how to help her, but the problem is that my business is still recovering from the pandemic. I offered to sell my house and move in with her, but she refused to hear of it."

I took a long drink of my beer. "I don't know what to do to help her," I said glumly. "I need to find a lot of money – fast."

"I have a great idea," Isaac said, waving his hands excitedly.

Gavin and I looked at him expectantly.

"Henry, you are a very handsome guy. Very good looking."

I looked at my best friend like he was crazy. "Um, thanks? But I don't see how hitting on me is going to help my problem."

Isacc rolled his eyes. "I know this guy who's been working as an escort. He makes like a thousand bucks a night or more, depending on the assignment."

"You think I should be a male prostitute to make money for my mom?" I asked incredulously.

"No, he's an escort, not a prostitute."

Gavin and I traded looks, both of us confused.

"An escort just accompanies ladies on dates. Apparently, there's quite a market for single older women who need dates for things like work events and family weddings, that kind of thing. According to my buddy, they need good looking, charming guys with good manners who can fake date these women."

"Fake date?" I asked. "This sounds like one of those movies my mom likes to watch on cable."

"Think about it Henry, it's perfect. You show up in a suit, go to the opera or an awards dinner or some shit, be charming, and four hours later you have a chunk of cash."

"Maybe I've had one too many beers, because that actually sounds like something that could work."

Isaac pulled his phone out of his pocket. "I'll text him and ask him for the contact information of the place he's working with. It's all very high class and they require a thorough background check and a full physical before they contract with you."

"Physical? I thought this was just fake dating?"

"It is, but just in case things go farther than intended, they like to make sure their guys are healthy."

I looked at my other best friend, seeking his counsel. Gavin nodded enthusiastically.

"I think this sounds great for you. Your hours are flexible with your company, so it'll be easy for you to shift things when a job comes up."

"Okay, I guess I'll check it out."

Liz

"Your mother is going to block your promotion? What a bitch."

"Evie," my friend Agnes chided. "It's not nice to talk about someone's mother like that."

Evie tossed her hair, the overhead light picking up the green highlights that were woven into her dark strands. The owner of Boozy Books was outrageous and had a 'take no shit' attitude that I admired immensely. I was glad that Agnes had encouraged me to join the book club.

"It's too bad you didn't find a chef after last month's book."

The Boozy Book Club was becoming famous for the way club members seemed to find love while reading books. When they read a mystery book, Evie had fallen in love with the police chief while investigating a mystery. Books about billionaires, bikers, and firefighters had all led to love for the women in the club. Even Agnes' story seemed to be connected to the club. After they'd read a baseball book, she'd met and fallen in love with Nolan, a player on the Seagulls.

It was particularly fun that most of the book club members were women in midlife, many of whom had given up on dating.

"Who got the chef last night?" Agnes asked.

"This new woman named Jane. It was her first meeting too. She left the meeting, went to a late dinner with a friend, and ran into a chef in the restaurant hallway."

We all looked at Evie in shock. It was hard to argue that was a coincidence. Besides, growing up around baseball players, I'd learned to be superstitious.

"Ooh!" Evie sat up in her chair, her eyes excited. "Maybe next month's book will help you, Liz. Even if you don't find love, it's an idea to help your situation."

I frowned. "I thought we were going to move away from romance books for a while."

The Boozy Book Club read a variety of genres, but the last few months had been strictly romance books, probably because half the women who came were hoping the book club would work its magic and send them love too.

"We are. Next month's book is a memoir about a male escort to the stars."

"Escort?"

"Yeah, he got paid to date some of the most famous singers and actresses. To be arm candy and act all lovey dovey with these women. You know, like when they needed a date and weren't actually dating someone at the time."

"Is that even legal?" Agnes asked.

"It's totally legal to be an escort," Evie confirmed. "You just can't pay someone for sex. In fact, there's an agency in the city that has both male and female escorts. I saw an ad for them when I made Jake take me to see *Mama Mia* last weekend."

"Oh yeah." Evie's friend Dawn spoke up for the first time. "How was that?"

Evie smiled. "It was great. For all Jake whined about going, I caught him singing along and – get this – smiling."

"Jake knows how to smile?" Dawn teased. The police chief was famously gruff.

"Sometimes. Anyway, you should check it out Liz. See if you can arrange for longer term escort. If your mom thinks you're serious about someone, maybe she'll step back and let you take over the Seagulls even if you aren't married yet."

"What if she finds out?" I asked. "Or worse yet, expects us to get married first? I have no desire to get married. Ever."

"Just string her along until your dad retires, then after you've got the job, you can stage a break-up. It's perfect."

Maybe Evie was right. If I seemed to be serious about someone, maybe that would get my mother off my ass, and I could go back to my nice, quiet life. There were no men that I knew that I was remotely interested in dating, either for real or for pretend.

I had my doubts if this would work, but I was out of ideas. When I was younger, I'd had a lot of guy friends I could have recruited for something like this, but now they were all married or in long-term relationships.

A stranger might be my best choice. And if I paid him, I'd have total control over the relationship. Maybe this could actually work.

***

The next afternoon I headed into the city to meet Mary Roberts, the owner of "Educated Escorts". According to their website, Educated Escorts specialized in escorts for professional people who needed someone sophisticated and well-read to accompany them to events.

Mary Roberts was an older woman, maybe mid-sixties, impeccably dressed and rocking sky-high heels and blood red nails. She had a strong, 'take no prisoners' attitude and I liked her immediately.

After she reassured me for the second time that my inquiry was completely confidential, I explained that I needed someone to date and potentially get fake engaged to for a few months. Mary didn't bat an eye, telling me that this wasn't the first time she'd been approached with this particular need.

"Most of my regular guys aren't available for a longer-term job right now," she explained. My stomach cramped in disappointment until she added, "But I do have a new guy you might like who would be open to something like this. His schedule is very flexible, and he's extremely smart and handsome. A little bit younger than you are though."

"How young?"

"He's thirty-five," she told me. "But younger guys are all the rage right now. Most of my clients are over forty, and increasingly they're looking for guys who make good arm candy as well as a good escort.

Plus, you don't look your age anyway, so it won't be as noticeable. Do you want to meet him and see if you click?"

"Click?"

"Well, you're not going to be able to pull off a fake relationship if there's no chemistry between you, dear. People notice that kind of thing."

"Oh, of course. When can I meet him?"

"Let me give him a call and see what his availability is."

Henry

I was surprised when Mary Roberts called me to say that she had a potential client to meet. I'd just cleared my medical and background checks yesterday. Even better, Mary told me that the client was looking for someone to pretend to be in a longer relationship with her. That meant a regular weekly paycheck I could use to help my mother get her treatments.

Since my schedule was flexible, I told Mary I could be at her office in an hour, saving my potential client another trip to the office. I took a quick shower, then put on black dress pants and a white dress shirt, open at the neck. I pulled on a blazer and black oxfords to complete the look. I briefly debated wearing a tie but decided against it. I hated those things.

The escort service office was only a short drive from my house. I still couldn't believe I was going to be doing this, but as Mary had stressed about a hundred times – and made me sign a contract agreeing to this – the service was strictly about dating and companionship. For my business I often had dinner or attended events with clients, in a way I guess this was the same thing.

Except I didn't pretend to be madly in love with my consulting clients.

The Educated Escorts office was sleek and modern, decorated in grays and whites with the occasional pop of color. The receptionist sent me up to Mary's office, where her assistant greeted me with a smile.

"They're in the conference room, Mr. James. Right that way."

I headed down the hall to the conference room, rapping my knuckles on the door before entering the room. And then I stopped dead.

Standing in front of the coffee station was a curvy goddess. She was on the shorter side, with lush curves barely hidden by the business outfit she wore. My eyes took in her full breasts, indented waist, rounded hips and strong looking legs.

My gaze fixed on the red high heeled shoes she wore before moving back up to her face. I had a flash of those heels digging into my ass while I pounded into her from above. I could scarcely breathe, I was too shocked by my reaction to her. I continued my perusal, eager to memorize everything about this woman.

Golden blonde hair reached past her shoulders in a sleek curtain, a slight wave giving it fullness. She had large brown eyes, a cupid's bow mouth, and a cute little button nose. On first glance I would have guessed she was in her early thirties, but as I stepped closer and noticed the fine lines at the corners of her eyes and mouth, I realized she was probably closer to forty.

The woman stared back at me, her expression of shock mirroring mine.

I'd never once had such an immediate reaction to a woman before. Some primal part of my brain was begging me to grab her, throw her over my shoulder, and take her back to my house.

Mary Roberts cleared her throat, drawing my attention away from the woman I was going to marry. Soon, hopefully.

"Henry James, I'd like to introduce you to Liz McNally, our client." She emphasized the word 'client'.

I extended my hand. "It's a pleasure to meet you, Liz."

She still hadn't spoken, but when she reached out her hand to meet mine, it felt like a good sign. I wrapped my fingers around hers, holding her hand just a little longer than necessary, as a steady hum of electricity moved between our palms. Liz frowned slightly, two tiny grooves appearing between her eyebrows as she stared at our hands.

Mary cleared her throat again, and we both pulled away. Liz visibly shook herself, then crossed to the other side of the room, putting the table between us.

"Usually, I suggest that for a longer-term engagement, the couple spend a little time together to get to know each other," Mary told us. "There needs to be a sense of intimacy or at least comfort with each other established before you present the escort as someone that you're in a relationship with. And you need to learn about each other and decide on an origin story."

"Oh, sure, that makes sense, Mary." Liz spoke for the first time, and her voice was smooth and throaty, like a good cognac. "Do you have time to grab a coffee or something, Henry?"

"Yes," I said, proud of myself for not suggesting that we grab a hotel room instead. "There's a shop across the street if that works for you?"

She nodded, then turned back to Mary. "If we, uh, hit it off, what's the next step?"

"You should both contact me separately through the confidential portal. If you want to hire Mr. James and he agrees to take you on as a client, I'll ask you both to fill out the escort contract. After that, you can set up engagements through the portal."

I guessed it made sense that Mary did not share people's phone numbers or email addresses with either side, even though working through the portal would be a hassle.

"Okay, I'll be in touch." Liz had the decisive tone of a woman who was used to being in charge. It only made me like her more.

She turned towards me. "Shall we?"

I followed her out the door, moving to walk next to her. When my palm settled at the small of her back, she jumped a little, but didn't pull away.

It was my first escort assignment, and I was already in big trouble. It had only taken one look for me to fall in love with my client.

Liz

My mind was racing as Henry and I walked across the street to the coffee shop. What on Earth was wrong with me? I'd taken one look at this guy – this younger guy, this guy who I was maybe hiring to date me – and my first thought was that I wanted to push him down onto the conference table and ride him like a freaking bronco.

I had never been so instantly attracted to a guy before. He was lovely. I know it sounded weird, but that was the word that made the most sense to me.

He was taller than me – of course most people were – and given that I only came up to just above his shoulders with three-inch heels, I was guessing he was about six two. He had broad shoulders that filled out the dark grey blazer he wore. Every part of him looked sturdy. He wasn't super bulky, but he also was clearly very fit.

His dark brown hair was highlighted with gold streaks that I knew came from the sun, not a salon. He wore it longer on top, shorter on the sides. His dark brows were almost straight lines above his almond-shaped brown eyes.

Henry had facial hair, although I wasn't sure how to describe it. It was too sparse to be a beard but too full to be scruff. I wasn't normally a fan of facial hair, but the second I thought about that beard/scruff/whatever scraping against my inner thighs I couldn't get the image out of my head.

"How old are you, anyway?" I asked as we walked into the café. I thought Mary Roberts had said he was thirty-five, but he looked younger than that.

"Thirty-five," he confirmed.

I shot him a suspicious look. "You don't look thirty-five."

"Thanks?"

"It's just that I'm worried no one will think we are really dating," I explained as we got into line to place our coffee orders.

"Why not?"

"Because you're just a baby compared to me."

"How old are you, grandma?" he teased, his eyes twinkling.

"Forty-five."

He raised his dark eyebrows. "Wow, I'd pegged you at forty."

"You think I look like I'm in my forties?" I screeched.

He stepped back like he was afraid I was going to hit him.

"Um. No?"

"Word of advice. A woman never looks older than thirty or thirty-five, unless she has white hair and orthopedic socks."

"Noted."

While we waited in the extremely long line we chatted easily. I bought us both a coffee and we retreated to a table in the corner to get better acquainted. As Mary promised, her escort was well educated and an interesting conversationalist.

"Is it okay if I ask if you have other jobs?"

Henry nodded. "I have a business consulting company. We do personality-based work."

"What does that mean?" I asked curiously.

"We use a series of personality tests like Myers-Briggs or the Strengths Test to determine an employee's communication styles, then we work on team building and relationships focused on understanding individual styles and working with their strengths."

"People pay you for that?" I said, before I thought better of it. "No offense, but that sounds kind of out there."

"Communication challenges and conflict are a source of constant problems in the workplace, especially now that people are returning to the office after the pandemic. But it's not just communication. By understanding people's personality types, managers can determine who should be given certain assignments and who will be successful with a promotion. There's a whole science behind it."

His passion for the topic was infectious, even if it all seemed kind of weird to me.

"And you do well with this work?"

He nodded slowly. "Business was really good before the lockdowns, then it ground to a halt. I'm slowly building it back up now."

"Is that why you need to do this escort thing?" I asked. "Because business is slow?"

His eyes clouded over, and he suddenly looked sad, making me feel like a jerk. Impulsively I reached across the table and covered his hand with mine, giving it a little squeeze.

"I'm sorry, you don't need to answer that, it's really not my business. I was just being nosy."

Henry shook his head. "No, it's okay that you asked. My mom is sick," he said softly. "She has breast cancer. They downsized her job, and she lost her health insurance. I want to make more money so I can help her keep getting the treatments she needs. She was a single mom and I'm an only child. She's all the family I have."

The pain in his voice broke my heart.

"I'm sorry Henry. It's ridiculous that health insurance is tied to employment in this country. And I'm sorry for prying. If you're going to be my fake fiancé, you should probably know right now that I tend to be nosy."

"Speaking of which, why on Earth would a woman like you need a fake fiancé?" His appreciative gaze made my nipples harden.

"We signed a confidentiality agreement, right?" I reminded him.

"Yeah."

"My family owns the Seagulls."

"You own birds?" he looked confused.

"No, we own the Seagulls, our local baseball team."

He scrunched his forehead. "We have a baseball team here? Hm. I don't think I knew that."

I studied him, trying to figure out if he was messing with me, but he seemed genuine.

"Yeah, it's a Triple A team. We're privately owned but we feed into the Atlanta MLB franchise."

I could tell by his face he had no idea what I was talking about.

"You're not a baseball fan, I take it?"

He shook his head. "I like football. Real football, NFL football, not soccer, just to be clear."

I recognized the vehemence of a fellow sports fanatic and couldn't fault him for it. I was mostly fixated on baseball myself, to the point I rarely followed any other sports.

"I'm the Chief Administrative Officer for the team and my father is the President and Chief Executive Officer. He and my mother own about eighty percent of the shares in the team, I own five, and a few outside investors own the remaining fifteen."

If he was impressed that my family owned a baseball team, he didn't let on. I appreciated that.

"Do you like your job with the Seagulls?"

I brightened. "I love it. I love baseball and I love the Gulls. I spent my childhood at the stadium and over the years, I've worked in damn near every admin job we have. I got my degree in Sports Management as well as an MBA. My career, my whole career, has been focused on taking over the Seagulls one day when my father retires. And now he's preparing to retire."

"So what's the problem? Sounds like you should be a shoo-in."

"My mother has decided that a forty-five year old woman who's never had a long-term relationship isn't stable enough to take over the team. She told me she'll vote against me to take over unless I get married."

Henry whistled. "Damn, that's harsh."

"It puts my father in the middle. He's groomed me to take over, but he also doesn't want to cross my mother. You do *not* want to get on my mother's bad side. I'm not sure if she's bluffing or not though. Like maybe she's just using the promotion as a way to blackmail me into 'settling down' as she calls it, as if a woman with a good career, a nice house, and a healthy investment portfolio isn't stable. It's infuriating, but I don't want to risk her going through with blackballing me. That's why I need a fiancé."

"Wow, your mom sounds so different than mine." His expression was sympathetic.

"I'm sure my mother loves me in her own twisted way. But the fact is, I'm my father's daughter and she's never been able to mold me into her own 'mini-me' and that just bugs the shit out of her."

"I'm sorry, Liz. That sounds hard."

"Well, not as hard as what you're going through with your mom," I pointed out. "Do they think she'll be okay after the treatments?"

He nodded. We sat in silence for a few minutes, lost in thought as we drank our coffees.

"When do we start?"

I reared back in surprise. "You still want to do this?"

"Pretend to be a beautiful woman's boyfriend to help her get the job of her dreams while simultaneously making money to help my mom? Of course I want to do this."

I stared at him for a long moment but saw no artifice in his handsome face. On the surface, he seemed like the perfect fake boyfriend. There was only one small problem: I was pretty sure I'd discovered that 'love at first sight' was real. Because the minute I saw him, I knew that I'd never be able to forget him.

I was probably playing with fire, fake dating a guy I was already having feelings for, but this was my best option right now. And Henry's too. Us fake dating could help us both get what we needed. I gave him a big smile and for an instant he looked almost dazed.

"Okay Henry Mason, let's get to know each other so we can kill this fake dating thing."

Henry

I gave myself one final once-over before I headed for the stadium. Today was my first official 'date' with Liz and I was joining her for a Seagulls game. I'd never been to a professional baseball game before and found I was looking forward to it. I'd even read up on the rules so I wouldn't look like a total idiot and embarrass my date.

Liz had sent me an official Seagulls jersey, telling me it would be a sacrilege to not represent the team when I was going to be sitting in the owner's box with her. I'd paired my jersey with faded jeans and sneakers, hoping that my casual attire wouldn't stand out too much.

It was a beautiful summer afternoon, warm but not too hot. A breeze was coming in from the water a few miles away, keeping things a little cooler.

As we'd agreed, my fake girlfriend met me outside the main entrance to the stadium. I was pleased to see that she was wearing jeans and a jersey as well, along with boots that added a couple of inches to her height. I wondered if she always tried to make herself taller.

We'd spent two hours together the other day rehearsing and getting our stories straight as we practiced for any questions that might come up today.

"Hi Sweetie."

Liz rushed towards me as soon as she saw me. She appeared to be alone, but I decided to take her lead, increasing my pace to get to her faster. She threw herself into my arms like we were long-lost lovers. Automatically my arms folded around her, and I hugged her tight, tucking her under my chin. The feeling of her curves pressed against me did funny things to my insides.

"Just in case someone is watching us," she whispered.

"Well, in that case, I think I should greet you like a real boyfriend."

Before she caught my meaning, I cupped the back of her head with my hand and leaned down to press my lips against hers. I meant to just make it a simple peck, a kiss of greeting, but the second our mouths connected my brain disengaged and my body took the lead.

Liz sighed against my lips as her arms came around my waist. Taking that as assent to continue, I licked my way into her mouth, my tongue tangling with hers. Soon a simple kiss became an intense make-out session that drew a few chuckles from people passing by.

She tasted like coffee and smelled like lavender, and I couldn't get enough of her. My body lit up with excitement, and judging by the way that Liz was grinding against me as she kissed me back, I wasn't the only one affected by this kiss.

When we pulled apart, Liz looked as shocked as I felt.

"Should I apologize?" I whispered against her lips.

She shook her head, then ran a hand down her hair. "God no. That was...that was something."

"Yeah, I liked it too. More than liked it."

We just stared at each other for a long moment before she seemed to come back to the present.

"We should probably go in before the game starts."

I held out a hand. "Let's go."

I spent the entire walk up to the box level obsessing about that kiss. I was pretty sure I was going to be thinking about it when I was eighty years old. I'd never had a kiss that was so immediately explosive. So perfect.

I wanted to do it again soon.

The owner's box was a large rectangle space with floor to ceiling windows looking down at the baseball field. Several rows of plush seats faced the window, and a few café tables and chairs were clustered in one corner. A buffet of delicious smelling food was set up on a table in the other corner, and there was a bar along the back wall, where a guy was pouring drinks for the guests. It was fancy.

As soon as we got inside, Liz introduced me to her friend Agnes, who was dating the Seagulls pitcher, a guy named Nolan. Apparently, it was his last season with the team before he moved into another job in the organization. Agnes's company was contracted to do publicity for the team, which was how they met. I knew from our conversation at the coffee shop that Agnes was one of Liz's best friends.

A few other friends and family of the players were in the box as well. The entire place had a relaxed atmosphere, with everyone seeming to know each other.

"Elizabeth?"

Liz stiffened beside me, and I squeezed her hand as we turned around. I knew without her saying anything that we were about to meet her mother. Liz had told me that she took after her father's side of the family, but it was almost shocking how different she looked from her mother.

Where Liz was all gentle curves and bright energy, her mother was sharp angles and cold as ice. She was tall, almost as tall as me, with a face that had obviously had many anti-aging procedures done on it. She looked younger than I knew she must be, but her face looked plastic and unmovable. It was kind of creepy. Unlike everyone else in the box who was dressed casually in Seagulls gear, Mrs. McNally was wearing an expensive white pantsuit and high heeled shoes that added several inches to her height.

"You must be Liz's mom," I said brightly, sticking out the hand that wasn't holding onto Liz. "I'm Henry."

Shaking Liz's mother's hand was like holding a cold fish. A limp cold fish.

"Elizabeth dear, you didn't tell me you would be bringing anyone to join us today."

Liz's voice was almost as icy as her mother's. "I wasn't aware that I needed your permission to bring a guest, Mother. It's never been an issue before."

I dropped Liz's hand and wrapped my arm around her shoulders, sensing that she needed comfort. Her mother's eyes followed my movement, squinting slightly as I pulled her daughter close to me.

"I didn't realize that you were seeing someone."

I couldn't decide if Mrs. McNally sounded suspicious or annoyed. Maybe a little of both.

Liz wrapped her arm around my waist and leaned into my side. "Well, I am."

"He's a little young for you."

"He's over eighteen, Mother, and my relationships are none of your business," she sniped. "Now if you'll excuse us, the game is about to start."

Liz led me to seats on the opposite side of the space, sitting as far away from her mother as possible. I made a mental note to tell my mother how much I appreciated her, because seeing Liz and her ice queen mother made me appreciate my own mother even more.

"Well, that went like I would have expected," Liz whispered. "At least she didn't have time to ask you about your net worth."

"There's still nine innings," I teased.

"Do you think she bought it?" she asked. "She seemed suspicious about our age difference."

"I don't know, but I have an idea."

"What?"

"How do you feel about a public marriage proposal?"

Liz

I ignored the flutter in my stomach at Henry's question, reminding myself that this was all fake. Despite that kiss. Holy crap that kiss. My panties were still wet from how quickly I'd become aroused.

In all my years of dating, I'd never been kissed like that. Henry kissed me like I was the oxygen he needed to breathe. He both cherished me and devoured me. And if my body reacted so strongly to a simple kiss, I couldn't help but wonder how it would react in other, more intimate scenarios.

He's ten years younger than you, Elizabeth Anne McNally, I told myself sternly. *Plus, you are paying him to be here. This is all an act.*

The problem was that somehow it didn't feel like an act. Not when Henry held onto my hand like he was afraid I'd leave him.

"I brought an engagement ring," Henry whispered. "I thought we could do a public proposal to make things seem real. If you're up for it."

I stared at him for a long moment, unable to decide if he was brilliant or crazy.

"It's our first date," I whispered.

"The first date they know about," he reminded me. "Remember, we've been dating for a few months now, and we're crazy about each other."

I'd almost forgotten the way we'd agreed upon a back story.

"Oh yeah. Okay, let's do it."

"When's a good time?"

"After the seventh inning stretch. Everyone always takes a little break then."

He nodded, then pulled me close and kissed my temple. "You got it."

Even though I was expecting it, the proposal caught me by surprise. I guess maybe I thought that Henry would change his mind. Right after we all sang *Take Me Out to the Ballgame* he stood up, turned to face me, and called out, "Everyone! Can I have your attention please?"

Once everyone stopped talking he continued, his voice strong and sure.

"Three months ago, I met the most incredible woman in the world. Every day since then has been a gift, and my mother always told me that when you find something precious, you should hold onto it with both hands."

He dropped to one knee in front of me and held out a ring box, flipping it open to reveal a beautiful sapphire ring.

"Elizabeth Anne McNally, will you please make me the happiest man on Earth and be my wife?"

Against my will, my eyes filled with tears. If I had scripted my own proposal, it wouldn't have been any better. I dropped to my knees in front of him, holding out my left hand.

"Yes, Henry Allen James, I will marry you."

He slid the ring on my finger, and somehow it fit perfectly. I stared at it for a long moment before I threw my arms around his neck and kissed him so long and hard that I felt his cock growing between us. I pulled back slowly, staring into his beautiful brown eyes and totally forgetting that this was fake.

Suddenly everyone burst into applause. People crowded around us, hugging me and shaking Henry's hand. My mother pushed her way through, looking almost happy with me for the first time in my entire life.

She grabbed my left hand, staring at the ring for a long moment. It was a beautiful ring, antique and obviously expensive. I liked it a lot. It looked perfect on my hand, and I was already sorry I wouldn't be able to keep it.

"Nice ring," she said to Henry. "Welcome to the family."

And then she pulled us into a hug. I was pretty sure the last time my mother had hugged me was when I was seven years old and broke my arm jumping off the roof of my father's Suburban on a dare. I didn't know what to make of it.

A little while later Henry went to the restroom and my friend Agnes dropped into the chair next to me.

"The Boozy Book Club strikes again," she said softly.

I looked around, but everyone else was focused on the game. Like I'd normally be, if I wasn't so distracted by Henry.

"What are you talking about?"

"Did you read our next book club book yet?"

"No, why? Isn't it an autobiography? Or a memoir? Honestly, I'm not sure what the difference is."

"It is a memoir, but at the end the male escort stops being an escort because he falls in love with one of his clients."

"Really?"

Surely that couldn't be true. It was too much of a coincidence. But then again, the book club had already had a lot of weird coincidences leading to love. I had seen it myself a couple of times now.

"Yeah. I know you were hoping to snag a chef, but this guy seems good too," she teased. "He's charming and good looking to boot."

I gave my friend a side hug. "He really does seem like a good guy."

"You'll end up together in real life," Agnes predicted. "I can see it in both of your eyes. You all are totally smitten."

I couldn't deny it.

My mother insisted that we all go to dinner with my father after the game. If I was totally honest, I didn't really mind lying to my mother about being engaged, but I did feel a slight twinge of guilt with my father. But there wasn't much I could do about it, not until I secured the President job with the Seagulls.

After a brief consultation, Henry and I agreed to meet my parents at their favorite restaurant. We had driven separately, but my car would be okay in the employee lot, so I followed Henry to his car.

"You did great," I told him as we slid into his late model BMW. "Everyone loved you and that proposal was perfect."

I held out my hand, admiring the ring.

"This ring is so beautiful. Where did you get it?"

"It was my grandmother's."

I almost swallowed my tongue. "Henry! You shouldn't give me something so precious to you. You don't even know me."

He turned to face me, his face totally serious. "I feel like I do know you, Liz. I know you here."

He tapped his chest, and I gasped.

Desperate to lighten the mood, I teased, "You don't have to act in the car. No one can hear us in here."

He took my hand in his, the familiar buzzing lighting up my skin.

"I'm not acting, Liz. You feel it too, right? This thing between us? It's like nothing that I've ever experienced. It's like the moment I saw you, I knew you were mine. Those kisses confirmed it."

My jaw dropped, a mix of emotions racing through my mind. I was thrilled. I was dubious. I was shocked. And most of all, I was confused.

"Are you messing with me right now, Henry?" I asked. "Because if you are, it's not funny."

"I've never been more serious about anything in my life. I like you Liz, I like you a lot."

"But you're so much younger than me."

"Ten years doesn't matter, not when we're this age," he said stubbornly.

"I'm paying you to date me."

"I'll tear up that contract right now, if you want."

It was tempting to say yes, but I knew he needed the money.

"But your mother needs your help," I reminded him.

"I'll figure something else out."

Henry reached up to cup my cheek and I couldn't help but lean into his touch.

"This is crazy. We've known each other, what? Four days? It's literally our first date! We're adults, adults don't act like this!"

"Answer me this. If everything else faded away...your mother, our age gap, the escort thing...if we'd known each other for months or years instead of days, what would you do then? What does your heart tell you?"

Our eyes met and held for a long time.

"My heart tells me you're a little bit crazy, and I've been missing crazy in my life."

One corner of his mouth quirked up.

"I'm not playing a game Liz and I'm not some guy who just falls in love with every hot blonde he fake dates."

He paused, his gaze raking up and down my body. "And make no mistake, you're the hot blonde in this scenario."

When I didn't respond, he added, "I don't know what's happening between us, and I know it's all happening crazy fast, but if there's one thing I learned from my mom being sick it's that life is way too short to let fear keep you standing on the sidelines. Just please, promise me that you'll be here with me. That we can at least explore whatever is happening between us and see if it's as real as it feels."

I had to be crazy, because I heard myself whisper, "I promise."

Henry

Proposing to Liz was a total mind fuck. I kept reminding myself it wasn't real, except that it felt real. Too real. I'd been worried ever since I met her that maybe I was making things up in my head. That there wasn't this connection between us. That I was being overdramatic when I felt like the love of my life had practically fallen into my lap.

But then we'd kissed, and I'd known it was all real. And when I looked into Liz's eyes, I knew without a doubt she felt it too. But she was scared. I sensed trust didn't come easy for her. She needed time, and I got that. I probably needed time too.

The two of us went to meet her parents for dinner. The restaurant was a little nicer than I'd expected given that Liz, her father, and myself were all dressed in jeans and Seagulls shirts. Mrs. McNally was dressed like she was going to a corporate board meeting, so she fit right in.

I could see that Liz took after her father. He was short for a guy, probably five seven or five eight, and his wife towered over him. He was built like a pit bull with wide shoulders and muscular arms. He was getting a little bit of a pot belly, but even I could see he was good looking with his silver hair, square jaw, and sparkling brown eyes.

We ordered a bottle of champagne and Mr. McNally toasted us. He seemed like a great guy, warm and funny. He'd acted surprised and maybe a little bit hurt when he heard about our relationship and my proposal to his daughter, but he was cautiously friendly. I could tell he hadn't made up his mind about me yet, and I had no doubt he was keeping an eye on me to make sure I didn't hurt his daughter. I respected the hell out of him for that.

Meanwhile Mrs. McNally was hinting around trying to determine my net worth. She was less than enthused when she realized that I was a lowly business consultant. Even Liz pointing out that I owned my own company didn't help.

"You'll sign a prenup of course. I'll have our lawyer start working on one."

"Mother! You will do no such thing."

"It's a commonly accepted practice in our social circles, Elizabeth." Mrs. McNally had a unique ability to make everything she said to her daughter sound like a rebuke.

"I don't care." Liz said in a firm tone. "My finances and my relationship with my fiancé are none of your business."

When Mrs. McNally opened her mouth to argue, her husband laid a hand on her arm. "Let's not talk business at dinner, darling. This is a celebration."

The rest of dinner passed quickly, then I drove Liz back to her car. She had a sweet little Mustang convertible, which seemed to suit her.

"I bought it for myself when I was promoted to Chief Administrative Officer," she explained. "People are always surprised when I say this, but I had to compete for the job, the same as anyone else."

"When's our next date?" I asked.

"Um, well, we should probably be seen around town, so our fake engagement seems realistic. You know, doing coupley things. Just enough so it gets back to my mother."

"So, we should go grocery shopping together?" I teased.

"Or pick out new curtains for my bedroom."

Heat bloomed on her face as we both pictured all the things that could happen in her bedroom. If that kiss was any indication, the two of us were going to burn up the sheets.

"I really appreciate everything you're doing for me, Henry. Even if the personal stuff doesn't work out, I want you to know that."

It would work out, I didn't doubt it, but I didn't want to push her any more today, not when it was technically our first date.

"I know this is against the rules, but can we exchange phone numbers? I hate talking to you through the portal and also, I would love it if you could text me to let me know you got home okay."

She studied my face as if she wasn't sure I was serious, then pulled out a phone from her purse.

"What's your number?" she asked. "I'll text you."

I rattled off my digits and a few seconds later my phone buzzed in my pocket.

"Thanks," I winked. "We just won't mention this to Mary Roberts at Educated Escorts. That woman scares me."

"Me too." Liz leaned forward and gave me a quick hug. "Good night, Henry."

I rolled down the window as she opened her car door. "Don't forget to text me please."

"Okay."

Liz and I went out five times in the next two weeks. Each time in public, making sure we were seen. In many ways this was a small town, and every time we went out, we ran into someone Liz knew from somewhere. She assured me that news would get back to her mother about our outings, reinforcing our story.

One night we went to the movies, sitting right in the middle and snuggling as we shared a giant tub of popcorn. Twice we went to dinner together, and once we shared breakfast at the local diner, fully aware that people would think we'd spent the night together. I also attended another Seagulls game with Liz, this time sitting in the stands where we could be with the regular fans and enjoy the sun.

We ended each date with increasingly passionate make-out sessions that I'd fantasize about every night when I went to bed. Or pretty much all day long, if I was being totally honest.

In between our dates we'd taken to texting each other a few times a day. I'd almost forgotten that we weren't dating for real until Mary Roberts called me. Liz and I had carefully avoided any mention of the fact that she was technically still paying me to date her. I think neither of us wanted to rock the boat.

"Mr. Mason," the owner of Educated Escorts greeted me. "How's it going with your client Liz McNally?"

For some reason it bugged me to hear Liz referred to as a client, even though it was technically true.

"It's going well," I said carefully. "We've been on several dates so far."

"Great, I need you to fill out your invoice on the portal so I can pay you. You must have missed the email I sent you about it."

I paused. On the one hand, I was having so much fun with Liz that it felt unethical to bill her. On the other hand, I needed that money for my mother's medical care.

"Ms. McNally has prepaid for three months," Mary continued, unaware of my conflict. "She seems pleased with your performance."

"Okay, great. I'll get to that today, Mary. Thank you for calling."

"Keep up the good work and you'll have a long history with us, Mr. Mason."

I couldn't decide how I felt about Liz prepaying for our dates. On the one hand, I appreciated the vote of confidence from a client. On the other hand, it made me wonder if she really just saw me as the hired help.

It wasn't like me to be insecure, but the nature of our relationship made everything complicated. I realized that in many ways the contractual part of our relationship was a no-win situation for both of us. If she continued to pay me, it would make things feel impersonal and transactional, as if our relationship wasn't real. If she didn't pay me, it wouldn't feel right either since that's what we'd agreed to.

The money made me conflicted, but Liz herself didn't. We were going for a hike tomorrow, and I couldn't wait to spend more time with her.

Liz

As I got ready for my date with Henry, it struck me how these fake dates felt more fun and engaging than any actual dates I'd been on. We'd been having a great time going out together, and we'd fallen into the habit of texting with each other for at least an hour before bed.

It all felt very real, despite the fact that I'd just paid an invoice to Educated Escorts. I'd gone ahead and pre-paid for three months, not wanting to have to deal with it every month.

Henry picked me up at my house. That was also against Educated Escorts rules, and I understood why the company insisted that clients and escorts didn't exchange personal information. But given that we were spending so much time together, it seemed unnecessary to communicate through the company's client portal. Not to mention the fact that it would seem weird for an engaged couple to always drive separately to their dates.

I opened the door to find Henry wearing khaki shorts, a tight navy blue tee shirt, and hiking boots. He looked edible. His scruff was a little bit scruffier today, like he hadn't trimmed it in a few days.

He took in my running capris and tank top, his gaze lingering on my breasts for a few seconds longer than was acceptable. I held up a tote bag as I exited the front door.

"I've got water, snacks, a jacket, sunscreen, and insect repellent."

"Wow, preparedness is so sexy on you."

He pressed me against the front door, giving me a long, lingering kiss. Suddenly Henry jumped back, looking around. "What the hell?"

"What's wrong?" I asked.

"Something scratched my leg."

He pointed down to where a red mark was rising just above the top of his hiking boots.

"Oh sorry about that, it's just Marvin."

"Marvin?"

"My feral guard cat. He gets a little protective. Do you want a bandage for that?"

He glanced down. "No, it's not bleeding so I guess it's okay. You have a feral cat named Marvin? How does that happen?"

He took my hand and led me to the car.

"I started feeding him last year. He really likes me, but it makes him anxious to be in the house. When I'm outside he'll be all affectionate, rubbing against me and sitting in my lap, but unless it's super cold he doesn't hang out inside. I think he believes he's supposed to protect me because he attacks anyone who gets near me when we're outside."

I slid into the passenger side of his gray BMW and waited for him to come around to his side.

"This has happened before?" he asked as he slid the key into the ignition.

"Oh yeah. The mail carrier and the UPS guy know better than to get close to me lest Marvin attack them. He let you off easy though, he must like you."

Henry stared at me.

"Don't look at me like I'm crazy. I only have the one cat. I can't help it if he's a little weird."

He shook his head, mumbling something I couldn't understand. But once we got out of the city and onto the quiet country roads he reached for my hand and held it all the way to the trailhead.

We set off on a five-mile loop that was labeled as 'moderately challenging'. Henry and I were in good shape, with both of us running and working out most days, so we figured it would be an easy hike for us.

"There will be fewer kids and dogs," Henry said when we talked about it. "Those easier trails get a little crazy on the weekend."

Little did we know that the 'moderate' hike was only moderate if you were an Olympian. By the time we'd finished climbing over giant fallen trees, wading across streams, and climbing steep hills we were both hot, tired, and sweaty.

"I guess I'm not in as good of shape as I thought," I said as we stopped to soak our feet in a stream about half a mile from the trailhead. The cool, clear water immediately cooled me down.

"This trail is definitely mismarked," Henry said. He took off his cap and filled it with cold water from the stream before putting it back on. Rivulets of water ran down his face as he grinned at me. He looked boyishly handsome.

"Thanks for being a good sport about it," he said. "A lesser woman would have been upset."

"I don't know if you noticed this about me Henry, but I'm no delicate flower."

He leaned forward and nipped the shell of my ear, sending shivers down my spine.

"Speaking of delicate flowers, I've been dreaming of licking yours. Every. Single. Night."

Heat raced through my body so fast I almost felt dizzy. Pushing to my knees, I shifted to straddle his lap.

"I wouldn't be opposed to that," I said coyly. "I always enjoy a good flower licking."

I didn't add that I'd been burning up my vibrator ever since I met him, imaging just that scenario, and many more. Thankfully the toy plugged into the wall, or I'd be needing to get a Costco size package of batteries to keep up with me.

"There's only one problem," I said, making my voice high and breathy. "We're not allowed to be together in real life. It's forbidden."

Henry wrapped his hands around my waist, sliding me closer until my core was pressed against his cock. He deepened his voice and went along with the game.

"Here's the thing, sweetheart," he mock growled. "I'm a bad boy. I don't care about the rules."

Our mouths crashed together, both of us eager to get closer. Henry smelled like a mixture of the outdoors and masculine perspiration, not that I smelled much better myself. That hike had been a bear. It was a good thing that I was pretty fit, or I would have totally embarrassed myself.

Henry's fingers tunneled into my hair, holding my head where he wanted it, while I gripped his strong shoulders. Between us I could feel his erection growing, and I couldn't help but grind myself against him, seeking friction.

The sound of voices finally broke through the haze of our passion.

"Should we head back?" I asked breathlessly as I removed myself from his lap. "I don't want to give any hikers a show."

He looked down and grimaced like he was in pain. "I'm going to need a few minutes."

I rolled my lips in to keep from laughing. The bulge in his shorts was impressive.

"It would help if you stopped looking at it, Liz."

This time I did laugh. But I turned to face the other direction, staring out at the slowly moving water until Henry was able to get to his feet.

Henry

My phone beeped just as we got back to my car, and I saw my mom's name on the screen.

"Sorry, I have to take this."

Liz nodded, stepping a few feet away to give me the illusion of privacy.

"Hey Mom, what's up?"

But it wasn't my mom who answered.

"Mr. Mason, this is Renee Stevens, I'm calling for your mother."

A wave of foreboding hit me like a brick to the head.

"What? Who are you, again? Why do you have my mother's phone?"

"I'm the hospital social worker at White Cross," the woman on the other end of the line said calmingly. "Your mother took a fall and was brought to the hospital by ambulance."

My heart stopped, and pure adrenaline raced through my veins.

"Oh no, how did she fall? Is she okay?"

"She's a little shaken up but she'll be okay. We're going to keep her overnight as a precaution. She wanted me to call and let you know."

I glanced over at Liz, who could obviously overhear the conversation. She gave me a sympathetic look.

"Okay, thank you. I'm a little bit away from town but can you please tell her that I'll be there to see her at the hospital as soon as I can?"

"I'll let her know Mr. Mason."

I ended the call and hung my head, staring at the ground as I tried to gather myself. Liz came over and wrapped her arm around me.

"Let me drive," she said quietly, leading me towards the passenger side of my car.

I handed her my key and got into the car without an argument. She was right, I was too freaked out to drive. When I heard that social worker's voice on the phone, I thought for sure I was about to get much worse news. I wouldn't be able to calm down until I saw Mom for myself and verified that she was okay.

"Which hospital are we going to?" Liz asked.

I loved the way she just assumed we'd go together. The truth was, I needed a friend for this.

"White Cross."

She nodded and pulled out of the parking lot. "What did they say?"

"All I know is she fell, and someone called her an ambulance. Supposedly she's going to be okay but they're keeping her overnight for observation." I paused. "Oh my God, the hospital bill."

"We'll figure something out," she said calmly. "Let's just focus on your mom right now, okay?"

The ride to the hospital seemed to take hours, but in reality, it was like forty-five minutes. The second Liz put the car in the park I shot out of the car and started fast walking towards the entrance to the hospital. Liz jogged to catch up with me, grabbing my hand.

"You need to be calm," she told me. "You don't want to freak your mom out, right? Take a breath."

I took a deep breath and blew it out, slowing my pace. After stopping at the check-in desk, we headed up to my mother's room. Mom was in a single room, looking tiny and frail in the white hospital bed. She was wearing a bright pink scarf around her head and had a cast on her arm. Machines beeped steadily behind her.

"Mom!"

I rushed forward to hug her.

"Hi, baby." She sounded tired.

"Are you okay? What the hell happened?"

Mom's gaze went behind my shoulder. "Oh, I see you brought a friend."

Liz stepped forward and gave my mom a friendly smile.

"Hi, I'm sorry to intrude. My name is Liz. I'm a...friend of Henry's. We were just coming back from a hike when Henry got the call from the social worker."

Mom perked up noticeably when she heard that news. "Hi Liz, I'm Henrietta, it's nice to meet you."

Liz's eyes moved between us.

"Yes," Mom laughed. "I named him after myself."

"I love that," Liz said.

Just then a doctor came in. He was wearing blue scrubs, a white coat, and a harried look.

"Ms. Mason?"

"I can wait outside if you'd like," Liz offered.

I grabbed her hand, threading her fingers through mine. If we were about to get bad news, I wanted to have Liz close by. I didn't want to analyze that right now though.

"Please stay."

When I turned my attention back to my mother, her eyes were fixed on our joined hands.

"I'm Dr. Mills, you must be her son."

I nodded.

"I was just coming to give your mother an update. Is it okay to talk in front of everyone?" the doctor asked Mom.

"Yes, of course."

"The good news is that your injuries are very minor. There is no evidence of a concussion, and other than a couple of bruises and your broken wrist, everything else seems to be fine."

"Thank God," I breathed.

"So, I can go home then?" Mom asked hopefully.

"No Henrietta, because of your other health complications, we're going to keep you here overnight, just in case something happens. If you do okay tonight, we'll release you first thing in the morning though."

"It's okay for you to release me now, doctor. I honestly feel fine, and it's so expensive to stay in the hospital. My son will stay with me at my house tonight and keep an eye on me, won't you honey?"

"Is Raymond Jennesy in the building?" Liz spoke up before I could respond.

The doctor sent her a look of surprise and caution. "The CEO of the hospital? I'm not sure."

"No problem, I'll just text him and see if he's around to say hi to an old friend."

Liz

Seeing Henry and his mom so worried about the cost of an uninsured hospitalization broke my heart. Fortunately, I had some connections that could possibly help.

Raymond was a good friend of my father's and his daughter and I had been best friends growing up. He was also a workaholic, so I wasn't surprised when he texted me back telling me that he was here in his office and that he'd come down to say hi.

I'd dropped his name and the fact that I had his personal phone number on purpose. The hospital was chronically short-staffed and one older woman could be easily overlooked. I was sure the doctor would stop at the nurse's station as soon as he left here and tell everyone that Henrietta was a VIP. She'd get the best care possible now.

"How did you fall, Mom?" Henry asked as I watched the doctor head right toward the nurses. When they all turned to look towards this room, I knew my suspicions were correct.

"I was going down the stairs to get the mail and I tripped on the step," Henry's mother answered. "It was stupid. I put my hand out to keep from face planting and then I heard my wrist snap."

"Were you dizzy?" Henry asked solicitously.

His mother patted his hand. "No dear, just clumsy."

"Elizabeth!"

Raymond Jennesy strode in wearing a designer suit that probably cost more than Henry's car. He was in his late sixties with all white hair but still fit and devastatingly handsome. I could see Henrietta eyeing him appreciatively. Not that I blamed her. If I hadn't grown up around him, I'd feel the same. The guy looked like a stock photo of a silver fox.

"Uncle Raymond, I'm so happy to see you. This is my friend Henry and his mother Henrietta."

"I'm pleased to meet you both. How are you feeling Henrietta?" he asked, taking in the cast on her arm and the scarf covering her bald head.

"I'm fine, sir. I just took a little fall. The doctor said I could go home in the morning. I was ready to go now, but he said he wanted to keep an eye on me."

"Uncle Raymond I was thinking about that new patient treatment fund you were telling me about," I started, widening my eyes at him to silently tell him to go along. "I was wondering if maybe Henrietta might qualify for it. She lost her health insurance when she was downsized at her job."

Raymond picked up on what was going on immediately.

"As a matter of fact Elizabeth, I think she might qualify."

He turned to Henrietta. "We have a donor who has pledged to cover expenses and specifically said they wanted those funds to go to female patients."

There wasn't a trace of artifice in his tone.

"Oh, I don't want any charity," Henrietta protested weakly. "That kind of thing is for people who really need it."

"Actually, I've got some unspent funds I need to use by the end of the month," Raymond said smoothly. "If we don't use them, we just have to send the money back, and I hate to do that. I'll send someone in to help you complete the application. The donor will cover everything."

I knew Raymond would cover it himself, although I'd try to give him money towards the cost.

"Well, if you're sure." She was smiling now.

"Absolutely, it's a shame to let the money go to waste if someone can use it."

He turned back to me. "I've got to get back to work but I'm so glad I got to see you. Come on over to the house for dinner sometimes soon, Barbara and I would love to see you and catch up."

"You got it, Uncle Raymond. Give her my love."

I gave him another hug, whispering "thank you" into his ear. When I turned back to Henry and his mother, the look of relief on their faces was palpable. I was grateful that I had a way to help them.

We hung out with Henrietta until the sun set and her eyes got droopy. After promising to come back in the morning, Henry gave her a hug and we headed back to the car.

"I love your mom. She's so sweet, and it's obvious how much she loves you."

I could hear the wistfulness in my tone. Seeing the easy love between Henry and his mother was heartwarming. I'd spent a lot of time with my father, but most of the time I felt like I was a buddy or one of his players. Dad wasn't big on affection or words, he believed you showed how you felt about people through your actions. And my mother, well, she'd always been icy cold. I couldn't help but wish I'd had a mother like Henrietta.

"She's pretty awesome," Henry agreed as he adjusted his car seat back to his preferred position. I'd had to pull the seat almost all the way to the steering wheel when I'd driven the car earlier. "I got lucky, I know."

His stomach growled.

"It's kind of late and we never got dinner. I don't think I'm up to going to a restaurant, to be honest. Should we drive through somewhere on the way?"

"I've got some stuff in the fridge I can make for dinner, I think. I can cook you something."

I have no idea what came over me, other than the strangest urge to take care of him. Or maybe I just didn't want our time together to end yet. Either way, we headed over to my house, where I promptly started the kitchen on fire.

Henry

It had been a full day. An unexpectedly challenging hike with Liz. Making out by the river. Getting that call from the hospital about my mother's fall. My day had been a roller coaster of emotions, positive and negative.

I was so glad my mom wasn't seriously hurt. I'd tried to convince her to move in with me, or me with her, when she got sick and lost her job, but she had stubbornly refused, insisting that we both needed our privacy.

After I heard they needed to keep her overnight for observation I had been freaking out about what would no doubt be a several thousand dollar hospital bill, and I knew Mom had been too. At least until Liz saved the day.

I guess it was nice to have a girlfriend who was well-connected. We probably never would have heard about that treatment grant otherwise. Pausing, I reminded myself that Liz was, in fact, not my girlfriend. Despite the fact that I was currently slouched on her couch while she cooked me dinner, she technically was still my client.

The idea left a bad taste in my mouth. We'd grown close enough that it felt wrong to accept money to date her. I would have paid *her* money to date her, that's how much I liked her. If I was honest, I loved her, just like I'd thought that first day. And my mother knew I loved her too, I could tell by the little smiles she kept sending me and Liz when we were at the hospital.

Mom and I had always been close. I was an only child. She had unexpectedly gotten pregnant with me during college and decided to raise me on my own. I'd never known my father. For as long as I could remember, it had been just the two of us against the world. Liz had fit seamlessly in with us though. She and Mom had been talking and laughing like old friends by the time we left the hospital.

"Oh shit!"

I heard Liz's cry of surprise seconds before the smoke alarm went off. I raced into the kitchen to find Liz ineffectually waving a dish towel at a flaming pot. For the first time since I'd met her, she looked frazzled.

"Baking soda."

"What?" She turned, sending the towel close enough to the flames that it ignited. She shrieked and dropped it on the pan, making the fire grow.

"Do you have baking soda?" I asked, making my voice clear and calm.

"In the fridge I think."

I found it immediately, partly because the shelves were basically empty. Her refrigerator seemed to only have condiments, yogurt, and a container of coffee creamer.

Gently pushing Liz aside, I poured baking soda on the flames, and when they died down, I used another towel to grab the pan and bring it to the sink. Liz opened a window to let out the smoke, and I reached up to reset the smoke detector. I rubbed my ears. That alarm was super loud.

She flopped into a chair dejectedly. "I can't believe this happened again."

"You've set your kitchen on fire before?" I asked.

"Not since last year. My friend has a restaurant, and she gave me some, I don't know, whatever I was trying to cook. She said I just needed to reheat it but somehow it started on fire. I have no idea what I did. Maybe it was the oil?"

I couldn't help it, I burst into laughter. "Elizabeth McNally, do you not know how to cook?"

"No, but I have many other talents," she said in a dejected voice. "It's one of many reasons my mother figured no one would ever marry me."

I spied a loaf of bread on the counter. After checking to make sure it wasn't moldy or something I suggested, "We could have peanut butter and jelly sandwiches."

I had seen the jars of ingredients sitting alongside the condiments in the almost-empty fridge.

"I guess that will have to do," she said ruefully. "It's what I would have eaten if I was alone anyway. I can open a bottle of wine with it."

"Sounds good."

I made us a stack of sandwiches and Liz dug up a bag of chips from a cabinet. We sat on the couch eating our simple meal, an old nineties sitcom turned down low on the television. Liz snuggled against my side, where she fit perfectly.

"This was a great day," she said softly. Then she stiffened. "Well, I mean besides your mom getting hurt. And me setting things on fire."

I laughed. "I knew what you meant."

"Remember what you said before, in the woods, about licking my flower?"

My cock twitched. "Yeah."

She turned around to face me. "I'm going to be brave here and put all my cards on the table."

I shifted sideways so we were knee to knee. "Go for it."

She ran a hand over her face, then took a deep breath. "I hope I'm not going to make a fool of myself here, but I like you, Henry. I really like you. I know that we've had this physical connection since we met, but now it's more. If we'd met some other way, I wouldn't hesitate to sleep with you."

I could feel my dick swelling at her words.

"In fact, I'd be begging you to fuck me. But the fact is, I'm paying you to date me, and I don't know for sure if, well, if how you act around me is how you feel, or if, well if it's all part of the service."

My heart thudded painfully in my chest. I thought I'd been crystal clear about how I felt about Liz, but I hadn't realized she was still wondering if it was genuine.

"It's not part of the escort service, sweetheart. I feel exactly the same way. The fact is, if we're putting all our cards on the table, I need to tell you that I'm falling in love with you."

I was lying of course, at least about the falling part. I'd already fallen head over heels in love with her, and my feelings were growing stronger by the day. But I knew it was complicated, at least until we worked through the barriers between us.

"But you're ten years younger than me." Liz was grasping at straws.

"Don't care. Remember? We had this conversation before."

She waved a hand in front of me. "And you look like this."

I imitated her action. "And you look like this. You're sexy as hell, Liz."

Her cheeks pinked.

"Am I being foolish here?" she whispered. "Everything inside me says that I should trust you."

"If you are being foolish, then we're both fools."

I leaned forward and pressed my lips against hers. For a moment we were completely still, then I cupped her cheeks with my hands and deepened the kiss. I poured all my emotions into that one kiss and when we pulled away, Liz looked as shell-shocked as I felt.

"I'm going to fire you as a client."

"What?" She shook her head a little, like she thought she hadn't heard me.

I picked up my phone. "I'm going to message Mary Roberts and let her know I don't want to be your escort anymore. I'll tell her to refund your money."

"No, I should tell her that I'm not interested in your services anymore."

"If you fire me, Mary won't assign me any more clients, and I need the money for my mom," I reminded her.

"Then don't fire me. We can just keep going like we have been. I pre-paid anyway."

I shook my head. "We can't have the money thing between us, Liz. If we're going to have a real shot at this, we need to come into the relationship as equals."

"You're right," she said. "Is it selfish of me to not want you to date other women?"

I nodded. "Totally selfish. But I like you being jealous. Don't worry, I'll only fake date them. I'll save my real dates for you."

I returned my attention to my phone, shooting off an email to my boss at Educated Escorts letting her know Liz and I were parting ways.

"There. You're officially fired as my client."

"In that case, let me show you to my bedroom."

"To pick out curtains?" I teased, remembering our conversation in the beginning.

She gave me a sultry smile. "I want to show you my flower."

Liz

I pulled Henry off the couch, leading him to the back of my house. It was on the smallish side, but it was close enough to the beach that I could hear the surf when my windows were open, which I loved. I made a good salary with the team, way more than most people in this area, but we were still just a Triple A team, so it wasn't like we were paid as much as staff with the Major League teams were.

When we reached my bedroom, I suddenly felt nervous. I couldn't say why. With age I'd become confident in my own skin, despite my mother's digs at me. Maybe I was nervous because this somehow felt more important than it had with any other guy.

It's because you have feelings for him, I reminded myself. *Actual feelings.*

We stood in the center of the room staring at each other for a long moment, until Henry reached for my tank top. He pulled it up a couple of inches before I stopped him.

"I'm forty-five," I reminded him. "I have the body of a forty-five year old."

In my mind's eye, I pictured Henry with young and perky twenty-somethings, girls with flat stomachs and breasts that weren't gravitating downward with every year.

"You have the perfect body. It's been keeping me up at night with my hand on my dick thinking about it."

My eyes widened at his crude words while arousal flooded my core.

"Okay then, let's do this."

I helped him get my tank top off, then removed my sports bra which thankfully had a back clasp like a regular bra. There was nothing sexy about getting out of one of those compression sports bras, that's for sure. My heavy breasts fell free, jiggling a little, and Henry leaned down to take one nipple in his mouth. I dug my fingers into his hair, idly thinking that he must have a good conditioner because it was super soft.

"Mmm."

His sound of pleasure vibrated against my breast as he licked and sucked. He moved to the other side, teasing my nipples into hard peaks before coming back to kiss me again. I reached between us, tugging his tee shirt up as high as I could, and when we pulled apart Henry practically ripped it over his head. His chest was a little hairier than I'd expected, I don't know why, and as I rubbed my hand over his lightly furred muscles, I decided that I liked it.

"Pants off," he ordered in a deep voice I'd never heard before.

I stepped back, sliding my capris off, and then my underwear, while Henry did the same. I couldn't help but watch as he released his cock. It bobbed up against his stomach, hard and angry looking.

When we were both fully naked, we flew back toward each other, our kisses turning urgent and hungry.

Henry walked me backward until my knees hit the bed, then tipped us over. We landed on the mattress with a soft bounce. I shimmied towards the center of the bed, and he watched me with a wolfish glint in his eye.

"I believe I promised you some licking," he said, pointing at my glistening sex. "Open up."

I parted my legs and he slid between them, forcing me open even wider with his shoulders.

"Beautiful."

He placed a kiss on the soft swell of my lower stomach, then another on my mound before opening my labia with his fingers. He licked me from bottom to top and I sighed happily at the sensation of his rough tongue abrading my sensitive folds.

Henry seemed content to keep licking me over and over again, working me into a frenzy until I grabbed his head to stop him.

"My clit," I gasped, desperate to have him focus where I needed him the most. "Please."

"Impatient, huh?" he teased.

I pulled his hair in warning, and he smirked before lowering his mouth right where I wanted him. He circled my little button, increasing the pressure until he was grinding it against my pubic bone with his tongue.

My body stiffened as I felt my orgasm approaching. I pulled on his hair again, hard enough that he grunted in pain.

"Henry, I want you inside me when I come."

"You got it, gorgeous."

He grabbed a condom that he must have tossed onto the nightstand when we were undressing, and I sent him a grateful smile. Birth control was the last thing on my mind right now. I was in perimenopause, so I wasn't even sure if I could get pregnant anymore, but better safe than sorry. Having a baby right now would be worse for my career than my mother was. Plus, Henry and I hadn't talked about things like test results.

Henry rolled on the condom and lowered himself until his cock pressed against my entrance. I lifted my legs, crossing my ankles behind his waist.

"Are you ready?" he asked.

"Yes. Please. I want you. Now!"

"Then we're on the same page."

Henry slid in slowly, not stopping until he was fully seated inside me. We both groaned at the sensation. I felt incredibly full as my body stretched to accommodate him.

"Move," I ordered the instant my internal muscles relaxed.

He lowered his head and kissed me deeply while he began thrusting slowly into my channel. I used my grip on his waist to leverage my hips up to meet him, the shift making him hit a spot deep inside me that made me go crazy.

"Henry!" I gasped.

And then I was coming, impossibly fast. My internal muscles were clenching and unclenching, my fingers gripping his shoulders and my heels digging into his ass as I rode out the waves of my orgasm.

Henry shouted my name, his rhythm faltering right before I felt the heat of his release inside me. He pushed in deeper, groaning loudly with each jerk of his hips until he'd emptied himself fully.

We both stilled, staring into each other's eyes before he pulled away to deal with the condom. I lifted one limp arm, pointing at the trash can on the other side of the nightstand, and then he crawled back into bed next to me, pulling me into his arms. I snuggled in close.

"Can I spend the night?" he whispered into my hair.

"You'd better."

Henry

Waking up with Liz right beside me was incredible. She was sprawled half on and half off my body, her cheek resting on my right pec and one leg shoved over mine. Trying not to disturb her, I reached for my phone on the nightstand so I could check my messages.

Last night we'd lasted about an hour before we had sex again, the second time even better than the first. Then we'd snuggled in bed eating goldfish crackers and rehydrating before falling asleep. If I was going to hang out with Liz, I probably needed to bring my own food because my girl clearly was as excited about grocery shopping as she was about cooking.

When I turned on my phone there was a text from my mom telling me I could pick her up any time in the next few hours. I shot off a response, feeling guilty that I hadn't thought about her once since the instant Liz had taken off her clothes. My now real girlfriend was definitely distracting.

Liz shifted, slowly coming awake. Propping her chin on my chest she gave me a sleepy smile that made my heart pinch.

"Good morning."

"Mm. Good morning, Henry." Her voice was scratchy with sleep.

"I've got to head out and pick up my mom soon," I told her regretfully.

"Of course you do. No one likes to be stuck in the hospital."

I loved that she didn't get upset that I needed to leave her like some women would. I debated in my head a few minutes before asking, "I was going to barbecue at her house tonight. Mom has requested my special barbecued ribs. No pressure at all, but we'd love to have you join us."

She looked like I'd just given her a million dollars. I wondered how often people did nice things for her in the rest of her life.

"If you're sure your mom won't mind. I'd hate to impose."

I turned my phone so she could see the last text from my mom. *Make sure you invite your lady friend.*

"Okay then, I'd love to join you."

"Great. I'll text you the information, we'll probably eat around six."

"That sounds good. Let me know if I can bring anything."

"Oh no," I teased her. "I don't need you doing anything else in the kitchen."

She smacked my chest playfully, then kissed me until I finally had to leave her bed. Ninety minutes later I was getting a full interrogation from my mother.

"I can't believe you didn't tell me you were dating someone."

"It's still kind of new."

"New or not, I saw how you two looked at each other."

"How did we look at each other?" I asked curiously.

"Like I'm going to see my baby get married before I die."

I sighed. "Don't talk about dying, Mom. Please."

"Why not? We all do it eventually."

"Mom!"

My mother reached over and stroked my hair like she did when I was a little boy.

"Okay sweetie, I won't talk about dying if you tell me every detail about your new girlfriend."

I spent the entire ride back to her house doing just that.

Liz came over to Mom's house later that night, looking delicious in a red sundress, denim jacket, and wedged sandals. She had a six pack of bottled beer in one hand and a tray of store-bought brownies in the other.

I knew that her family had way more money than mine did, but she wasn't flashy or snobby, which I appreciated. And after meeting her parents, I was surprised that she was so normal and down to Earth.

"As soon as I'm feeling better, I'll need to start looking for a job," Mom was telling Liz as we ate our way through a ridiculous amount of ribs.

I'd grilled corn on the cob and baked some potatoes in foil to go with it, but the ribs were definitely the star of the show, thanks to my special sauce. Mom ate more than I'd seen her eat in almost a year. I was glad her appetite was returning despite still receiving chemo.

"What kind of work did you do, Henrietta?" Liz asked.

"Nothing exciting, I was a bookkeeper at a small accounting firm."

Liz's face turned speculative. "You know what, we have a part-time job open on the Seagulls accounting team right now. It's twenty-five hours a week and comes with insurance. We have very generous benefits at the organization. I wonder if you'd be interested in it."

"Liz," I said warningly.

I was pretty sure that the "treatment fund" she and her uncle had talked about at the hospital was a thinly disguised attempt for one or both of them to pay my mother's bill. Honestly, I was afraid to ask. If it was fabricated, it was hands down one of the nicest things anyone had ever done for me or my family, but then I'd also feel compelled to pay them back. And there was no way I could do that anytime soon with everything else going on.

"What's wrong, Henry?" Liz looked at me quizzically.

"You don't need to make up a job for my mom. We'll be okay. I can help her until she gets on her feet."

"I'm not making up a job," she protested.

I raised my eyebrows at her, and she sighed theatrically. "I've never seen this stubborn side to you before Henry and I have to say, it's not your best look."

Before I could respond to her rebuke, she opened her phone and after a few clicks, slid it over to me. It was the Seagulls webpage and job listings.

"We just opened this position yesterday. We had a stay-at-home mom in the job for years and it was perfect for her, but now that her kids are grown, she took a promotion into a higher-level full-time job."

I handed the phone to my mom, who scanned the listing. "I have all the qualifications for this job. I'll have to talk to my doctor, but I'm certain he'd release me for part-time work."

Mom looked hopeful and a little excited, which warmed my heart.

"I can't get involved in your hiring since we have a personal connection," Liz told her, but her gaze was on me. "I'm glad to put a good word in for you, but if you get the job, it will have to be on your own merit. No guarantees at all."

"I understand, dear. I wouldn't feel right about any special treatment anyway. Thank you so much for letting me know about this."

I hopped out of my chair and grabbed Liz under the arms, pulling her up to standing. Then, right in front of my mother, I kissed the stuffing out of her.

Liz

"I don't understand why we can't send out the engagement announcements."

I put my phone down and lightly pounded my head against the dining room table. My mother was driving me bonkers about my supposed engagement. She was set on the idea that Henry and I would have some huge society wedding, with me in some giant fluffy white monstrosity of a dress. I knew this because she kept emailing me links to her Pinterest boards for the wedding.

Even if our engagement had been real, there was no way I wanted a big wedding. Or a wedding dress that made me look like a cake topper. Nor did I want to spend time browsing Pinterest.

"Elizabeth? Are you there? What's that pounding?"

I put the phone on speaker without lifting my head.

"Mother, I'm going to tell you this for the very last time. Henry and I will arrange our own wedding. It will be small. It will be private. And I will not be wearing white like some twenty-two year old virgin."

My mother sighed in exasperation, like I hadn't been telling her this exact thing for three solid months.

Now that Henry and I were dating for real, I wasn't sure what to do about the engagement issue. I was pretty sure we could both see a future for us, but this early in the relationship, there was no way I was going to bring up the M word. I wasn't even sure I wanted to get married at all, to Henry or to anyone.

"But—-."

I cut my mother off. "If you bug me about the wedding one more time Mother, I swear to God we will elope to Las Vegas and get married by an Elvis impersonator. Then I'll put pictures up on the team's Facebook page too so everyone can see."

She gasped loudly, clearly horrified at the idea.

"Don't push me Mother, you know I'll do it."

"You're impossible Elizabeth." It was time for my mother's martyr act to start. "I don't know what I ever did to deserve a selfish daughter like you."

"Why don't you make a list of all your sins and that'll give you an idea," I suggested as the front door opened. "Henry's here, I've got to go now. Bye."

I hung up before she got another word in.

Henry walked in wearing a navy blue suit and looking all kinds of delicious. My now real boyfriend had a date with one of his clients tonight, and he'd told me that it would be his last one. His mom had gotten a job with the Seagulls and the accounting team was thrilled with her work. Even better, her employer sponsored health insurance had started a few weeks ago. Henry had accepted a few more assignments from the escort service to pay off the rest of the outstanding medical debt, but after tonight he was free and clear.

"How was your date?" I asked, walking over to give him a hug.

He grimaced. "She got a little grabby at the end."

I reached around and squeezed his ass. "Well, you are pretty damn grabbable."

"I found out tonight she'd also paid for me to go to some charity dinner with her next week, so I'm going to need to hold off another few days before I give Educated Escorts my resignation. I don't want to leave Mary in the lurch."

"What's the charity?" I asked.

"Honestly, I didn't even bother to ask. All those events are the same."

"True." I grabbed him by the tie, feeling a little bit possessive. "Did you tell your date to keep her mitts off my man next time?"

This time it was Henry who was grabbing some ass. He pulled me tight to him, roughly kneading my butt cheeks, and I could feel his erection growing against my belly. My nipples followed suit.

"I told her I had a very jealous girlfriend," he confirmed. "I don't think she believed me though."

"Silly woman. When's your next date?"

"Tuesday. And then I'm done for good with this escort gig, I promise."

"It's all good, and I won't be home Tuesday night anyway. That's my book club night."

Since Henry and I were spending almost every night together, I'd started to miss him when we couldn't be together. I still hung out with my friends, and he hung out with his buddies Gavin and Isaac, but when we didn't have anything pressing to do, we spent the evenings together.

I'd never miss book club though. It was the highlight of my month.

Once Evie found out that I was real dating my escort, she was over the moon about another romantic success from her book club. Agnes and I both had to remind her sternly, several times, that I did not want the truth to get out about how Henry and I had started dating.

For her part, Agnes had been a bit smug about it, reminding me that when she watched Henry propose to me at the ballpark, she knew then that we were really going to fall in love.

Love. We hadn't said the words, but I certainly felt them. I wasn't sure about Henry, but I was pretty sure that he was in love with me too. He'd told me before that he was heading in that direction. I wasn't one of those super mushy women. Henry showed me his feelings through his actions, and all the other sweet things he said. I didn't need some official declaration of love to feel confident in our relationship.

"This will be my last date for sure," Henry promised me again. "I told my date that I was getting out of the business after this because I had more important things to do."

"Yeah? Like what?" I teased.

"You."

He walked me around until my back was against the wall between the kitchen and the front door. My heart started pounding in my chest, the way it always did when I was this close to him.

"Whatcha doing?" I asked coyly, looking up at him from beneath my eyelashes.

"I missed you."

His mouth crashed down on mine before I could respond. His tongue swooped into my mouth, claiming me, and I was immediately wet. In the back of my mind, I wondered if it would always be like this. If my body would light up every time he touched me, even if we were together for the rest of our lives.

Henry grabbed my thighs and boosted me up, pressing me into the wall with his pelvis. I wrapped my legs around his waist and ground myself against his cock, immediately feeling desperately needy for him.

Henry pulled back enough to shove the neckline of my pajama top down, baring my breasts.

"I missed you most of all," he joked, as he boosted me up higher on the wall and wrapped his lips around my nipple. His tongue laved me, making my nipple painfully engorged.

"Henry," I gasped. "I need you. Now."

My hands slid down, trying to reach his zipper. He set my feet on the floor long enough to do it himself, dropping his pants and underwear to his knees before lifting me up against the wall again. He slid the crotch of my sleep shorts over with his fingers and without hesitation, speared me with his thick cock.

"Ahh."

I was too full to form words. I loved the feeling of having him inside me. I couldn't get enough. He started pumping in and out of my pussy, his slick skin rubbing against my insides in the best way possible.

A few weeks into dating we had the birth control talk. We'd both been tested and since I had an IUD, we'd agreed to go bareback. It had only made everything better. We'd also exchanged house keys and had taken to switching back and forth between our two houses, spending most nights together. I loved waking up in his arms every morning.

"You're squeezing me so tight, baby," he grunted, shifting me again until his dick hit my special spot.

I immediately felt the first flutters of my orgasm, and so did Henry because he started pounding into me like a man possessed. When my head started bouncing against the drywall, he slid his palm behind me and cupped the back of my head to cushion the blow.

"Henry!" His name was ripped from my throat as my entire body stiffened for an instant. And then I was coming, quivering around him as I took my pleasure.

Henry was only a minute or two behind me. I was still trembling with aftershocks when he groaned my name and pushed in deep, painting my womb with his warm seed. I loved feeling him fill me up like this, his hips snapping against mine as he released several long spurts of cum.

His knees gave out and we slid to the floor, our bodies still connected as if we couldn't bear to be apart yet.

Henry gave me a sweet smile.

"Well, that's something that's worth coming home for."

Henry

I hated these charity events. Over the years I'd gone to dozens of them for my business and since I'd been moonlighting at Educated Escorts, I'd gone to even more. If I had to sit through long boring speeches while eating tasteless chicken dishes, I wish I could at least have Liz here with me.

Liz. I was desperately in love with her. I hadn't said anything to her yet, afraid she'd freak out. But then again, things between us had been close to perfect. I was pretty sure she trusted me now and would believe me when I told her that I was all in for this relationship. I wanted nothing more than to make our fake engagement real.

"It's too bad you're not going to be doing these events anymore." Myra Simonson, my date for the evening, leaned close to whisper into my ear. Her heavy perfume was cloying and her artificially enhanced breast pressed firmly against my arm. It did nothing for me.

"You're the perfect date, Henry. Handsome and interesting."

Myra was the widow of some wealthy businessman I'd never heard of. The guy had been dead for a couple of years, and I had no idea why she was paying people to date her. She was rich, cultured, and beautiful. She would have no trouble getting a date the regular way. She was also a little bit of a shark.

Her hand slid up my chest and she placed a kiss on the side of my jaw. It was all part of the act, but it still made my skin crawl, probably because on our last date she'd tried to kiss me when I drove her home. A kiss on the cheek during a fake date to keep up appearances was one thing, trying to climb into my lap and suck my face off when we were alone was something else entirely.

"Henry!"

I stiffened, recognizing that icy cold voice. Shit. It was Liz's mother.

"What's going on here?"

And her father too.

My mind raced, trying to decide what to do. I couldn't out Myra. My contract with Educated Escorts clearly specified that violating a client's confidentiality would be grounds for being sued. I had no doubt that Mary Roberts would come after me and sue the pants off me if I embarrassed one of her best clients.

"Oh hello," Myra said coyly. "I'm Myra Simonson. I see you've met my boyfriend, Henry."

Mrs. McNally looked stunned, while Mr. McNally's face was turning a bright red, like his blood pressure was rising quickly.

"You're cheating on Liz?" he growled. "You have a lot of nerve, buddy."

"Who's Liz?" Myra asked.

"His fiancée," Mr. McNally spit out.

He was vibrating with anger, and I wished I could put his mind at ease. But I couldn't. Not here.

"That can't be right," Myra said, as if the idea that I was engaged was ludicrous. "Henry's my boyfriend."

I was going to kill her. I understood that she wanted to keep up appearances, but she also knew that I was seeing someone. I'd just told her that a few days ago on our last date when she'd broken the rules and gotten grabby. Right now, I was kicking myself for not quitting this job sooner. If I'd stopped after my last date with Myra this never would have happened.

I met Mr. McNally's eye. "It's not what it looks like. I can explain, but not right now. Not here."

"There's nothing to explain," Mrs. McNally said frostily. "You're clearly using our daughter, you slimy bastard. I knew there had to be a reason why someone so young and handsome would be interested in Elizabeth."

"Hey," I said sharply. "Don't you insult Liz."

"You insulted her when you cheated on her," her father snapped. "And watch how you talk to my wife."

Myra wrapped her hands around my biceps.

"Henry dear, I don't know what's going on here, but we need to go find our seat. The program is about to start."

I was too freaked out to do anything but follow her. Before I got two feet away, Mrs. McNally sank her talons into my arm, stopping my progress.

"Elizabeth is going to hear all about this, you money-grubbing asshole," she hissed. "There's no way she's going to marry you now. I will ruin you."

The second I got to the table, I pulled out my phone.

"What are you doing?" Myra whined. "I don't pay you to take personal calls."

Ignoring her, I typed out a few quick messages to Liz, warning her about what happened and letting her know that I'd stop by tonight after I got done with my obligation to Myra.

I hoped we could fix this with her parents. I just wasn't sure how.

I could see Mr. and Mrs. McNally a few tables over, glaring daggers at me. I was glad that the idea that someone was cheating on their daughter wasn't enough to tear them away from whatever the hell charity we were here to support. Seeing their eyes on us, Myra seemed to be purposely playing things up, whispering in my ear and touching me all through the interminably long dinner.

Finally, finally the stupid event was over. Myra wanted to stop at the ladies' room before we drove home, so I waited in the hallway, checking my phone. Still no response from Liz. I texted her again, wondering why I hadn't heard back yet.

When I looked down the hallway, I saw that Liz's parents were leaving as well, looking like two people on a mission. I felt a twinge of anxiety in my stomach. The whole situation was making me nervous. But I hadn't done anything wrong. I knew that, and Liz knew that. We'd fix this. Together.

I had to get home and find Liz as soon as possible.

Liz

I knew something was wrong the minute I got home. I'd left my phone on the kitchen counter and ended up hanging out with some of the girls after book club, knowing that Henry would be home late anyway.

Funny how I considered this his home as much as mine now.

I walked in the door, looking for my phone to see if I'd missed any messages. My jaw dropped as I saw that I had over thirty messages, from both of my parents as well as Henry.

"Jeez, what is going on?" I wondered.

Before I could read any of the messages, I heard someone pounding on the door. To my shock, my parents were on my doorstep, both dressed up like they were coming from some event. My mother looked immaculate as always in a long ivory dress made out of some shimmery material that hugged her slim curves. Dad was wearing a black suit, but he'd loosened his tie.

"What are you two doing here?" I asked. They'd been to my house maybe twice in the last ten years. "Did someone die?"

"Someone is going to die when I get my hands on him," Dad muttered, pushing past me into the room. I'd never seen him look so angry.

My mother swept in after him, her ice princess glare firmly in place as she looked around my living room like it disgusted her. For the record, my living room was very clean and comfortable. Mom had never liked the fact that I chose to get a comfortable little bungalow near the beach instead of living in some fancy condo downtown.

Before I could ask again what was happening to bring my parents here unannounced, I heard the key in the lock. Henry rushed through the front door, his eyes bouncing between me and my parents. Before anyone said a word, my father stalked over to Henry and to my horror, Dad punched him in the face.

"Asshole," Dad growled as Henry's head snapped backward with a sickening thump.

I rushed to my boyfriend. "Oh my God, Henry are you okay?"

Before he could answer I turned on my father. "What the hell is wrong with you?"

Henry rubbed his jaw. "Let's all calm down and discuss this like civilized adults."

My father moved towards Henry again, and I threw myself between them, placing my palms on his chest to keep him from hitting Henry again. He was lucky that my boyfriend hadn't hit him back. Henry was much stronger, younger, and significantly fitter than my father was.

"Please, can we all sit down and discuss this like civilized adults?"

When no one answered I said, "Mother, go into the kitchen and grab the bottle of bourbon off the top of the refrigerator, and bring back some glasses to go with it. They're in the cabinet to the right of the sink."

My mother looked affronted at my order but stalked off towards the kitchen anyway.

"You," I said pointing at my father. "Sit there." I shifted to point at a chair at one end of my six-person dining room table.

I grabbed Henry's hand and pulled him to the opposite side.

"Do you need ice for your jaw?" I asked.

He shook his head, looking miserable. My mother returned, pouring us each a drink without being asked to, then settling into a chair next to my father. I nudged Henry's glass towards him, then took a drink of my bourbon.

"Now someone please tell me – calmly and without any physical violence – what happened tonight."

"This asshole is cheating on you, Liz," my father growled. "He didn't even try to hide it."

"We saw him at a charity event with some low class wanna be trophy wife hanging all over him," my mother added, her voice full of venom.

Then she turned the venom toward me. "I knew this guy being interested in you was too good to be true. His other girlfriend is much younger and thinner than you. If you'd just lose a little weight..."

"Mother!" I exploded.

"Hey, don't insult my fiancée!" Henry yelled at the same time.

I looked at Henry. "Start from the beginning, please."

He looked at me then looked at my parents. "The confidentiality agreement," he murmured.

I was starting to put the pieces together.

"Mother, Dad, we can clear this up, but I need to have your word that you will keep what we are about to tell you confidential. What we share with you tonight will not leave this room and you will never use it against Henry or anyone else, ever."

They both nodded, but this wasn't my first rodeo.

"I need to hear the words. Dad, do you swear on your shares of the Seagulls?"

"Yes." He didn't look happy about it. "I will keep it confidential, whatever it is."

"Mother, do you swear on your diamond tiara?"

"Your mother has a diamond tiara?" Henry said incredulously.

My mother had a lot of expensive and useless crap, but her tiara was her pride and joy. If there was a fire, she'd probably save that stupid tiara before she'd save me.

"Not the most important thing right now," I mumbled. "Well, Mother? Do we have your promise?"

"Yes." Her tone was so icy I was surprised frost didn't build up on my table.

"Okay then." I looked back at Henry, and he nodded, giving me permission.

"Henry's mother has been very sick with breast cancer. Her old company fired her because she was costing their health insurance plan too much money."

"They can't do that," my mother said confidently. "It's against the law."

"Actually, it's not," Henry corrected her. "I know because we consulted a lawyer. All they have to do is make up a different reason to eliminate someone's position, like a layoff or restructuring, and it's legal even if we know it was about insurance costs."

"That's terrible," my mother said with a rare flash of empathy. "How is she now?"

"She's doing a little better. Thank you for asking. She just had her final chemo treatment."

"But what does your mother have to do with you cheating on my daughter?" my father asked, his eyes still filled with venom.

"Henry has been working at an escort service to make extra money to help pay for his mother's care after she lost her health insurance."

"You're dating a gigolo, Elizabeth?" My mother's empathy limit for the year had clearly been met. "That's tacky, even for you."

I sighed, and Henry squeezed my hand supportively.

"I'm not a gigolo, I'm an escort," Henry said firmly. "Educated Escorts has very strict rules about sexual activity between escorts and clients and it's strictly forbidden to sleep with the clients."

My father looked like he couldn't decide what part of this story to be mad about.

"Are you going to be dating other women for money after you marry my daughter?" he finally settled on.

Henry shook his head.

"No sir. Tonight was my last assignment. My mom's medical bills have been paid off, and she recently started a part-time job that offers both a good salary and health insurance."

"Wait, is your mother Henrietta, the lady who just started working in accounting at the Gulls? Her last name is Mason too."

"Yes."

"Oh, so this is the same woman you were visiting in the hospital when you saw Raymond, is that right Liz?" My father was connecting all the dots.

"Yes, that was her," I answered.

"Did you know about this escort thing all along then?" he asked me.

"Yes, Dad. I knew Henry was moonlighting at Educated Escorts."

I prayed that they wouldn't ask me if I'd ever hired Henry. I didn't want to lie to them, but I also knew that my mother would hold that against me until the day she died if she found out. Clearly Henry read my mind because he said, "Did Liz ever tell you about how we met?"

Henry

I knew Liz was worried about her parents continuing to ask questions, so I told them the same story I'd told my mother. It was the closest to the truth I could get without disclosing the part about Liz hiring an escort service.

"I was in this coffee shop in the city, and you know how it is, there's always a long line in those places. I looked up and saw Liz walk in the door and my heart stuttered in my chest. She got in line behind me, and I started talking to her, and by the time we finally made it to the front of the line, we were chatting like old friends. We had our coffee together and hung out for hours talking and laughing. Then I asked for her phone number, and the rest is history."

I wrapped my arm around Liz's shoulders, and she leaned into me, placing her hand on my thigh. Her father visibly relaxed.

"No more going out with other women, right?" her father asked.

"No more," I promised, meeting his eye.

"It's terribly embarrassing for me to have my daughter's fiancé going out on dates with other women," Mrs. McNally said disdainfully.

I could feel Liz rolling her eyes without even looking at her. "That's right Mother, it's all about you."

"I just don't understand why a pretty gal like Myra Simonson needs to pay for a date," Mr. McNally said.

"No idea," I responded. "I don't ask my clients anything personal and she never volunteered anything."

"I mean, looking like that, she can get her own dates," Mr. McNally continued, seemingly oblivious to the daggers that were shooting from his wife's eyes.

"You think that cheap floozy is pretty?" his wife asked angrily.

Mr. McNally shifted closer to his wife, grabbing her hand.

"No woman is as beautiful as you, darling."

He leaned forward and pressed a quick kiss on her lips, which seemed to pacify her.

Liz cleared her throat impatiently.

"Well, now that we've cleared everything up, how about you two go away now and leave me with my fiancé."

"Gladly." Mrs. McNally stood up quickly, as if she couldn't wait to leave. "Let me know if you want me to give you the number for my decorator, maybe she can do something with this place."

Her expression said it was doubtful. The woman really was a piece of work.

I squeezed Liz's hand to keep her from punching her mother or something. I rubbed my sore jaw. There'd been enough punching for one night, and Mr. McNally had a surprisingly strong right hook. My jaw was still throbbing.

We finally got rid of Liz's parents and settled on the couch to have another drink.

"Well, that was quite the drama," she said wryly. "Thanks for not outing me on the escort thing."

"It's all true you know."

"What?" She paused with her glass of bourbon in front of her mouth.

"The minute I saw you, my heart stuttered in my chest and when we were in that coffee shop talking, I realized that I was in love with you. I've fallen a little more in love with you every single day."

"Really?"

"Really."

She turned to face me. "I love you too Henry, I have from the start. I told myself I was just imagining it, that a guy like you could never be interested in a middle-aged woman like me."

She held up her hand as I tried to interrupt.

"Then I realized that it doesn't matter how old we are, all that matters is what's inside here."

She placed one hand on her heart, the other on mine.

"For whatever reason, we found each other Henry, and we just fit. I'm not willing to throw that away."

"I'm glad to hear you say that," I responded. "Because I want nothing more than to get engaged for real."

I grabbed her hand and pulled my grandmother's engagement ring off her finger, holding it up between us.

"Elizabeth Anne McNally, love of my life, will you make me the happiest man on Earth and marry me for real?"

She smirked as I mimicked our first proposal.

"Yes, Henry Allen Mason, I will marry you for real."

I slid the ring back on her finger, then pulled her close and kissed her until we were both breathless.

"Do you want to go have engaged people sex?" she asked when we pulled apart.

"More than anything."

Epilogue – Liz

One year later...

"Congratulations, Madam President."

Henry pulled me into a big hug. My father had announced his retirement today, as well as my promotion to be the new President and CEO of the Seagulls organization. The investors' vote had been unanimous, with even my mother supporting me for the role.

Reporters swarmed around, interested in talking to one of the few females in the job, but I ignored them for now. I'd already given a statement, and our communications team would set up some time for me to meet with them for interviews later.

"I'm so happy for you dear."

Henrietta gave me a big hug, her short gray hair glinting in the light. She was officially cancer free and looking much better than when I'd first met her. Her hair was growing back, she'd gained some weight, and she was thriving in her job with the Seagulls.

I relaxed into the hug, grateful for the easy affection she gave me while my own mother stood by awkwardly. We'd gotten really close over the last year, enough that Henry liked to grouse that his mother liked me more than him. It was probably because we never invited him to join us for our spa days.

Henry and I had got married six months ago in a small ceremony on the beach. Only my parents, Henrietta, Henry's friends Isaac and Gavin, and my best friend Agnes and her fiancé Nolan were present.

Nolan had retired from the Seagulls at the end of last season after a super sweet public proposal, and soon I'd be standing up in his and Agnes' wedding the way she'd done for me.

After months of nagging, Henry and I had broken down and agreed to let my mother throw us a small party the week after the wedding. Two hundred people were there, as well as several society

"

reporters. My mother had used it as her chance to shine, bringing in a string quartet and gourmet appetizers.

Henry, his mother, and I had snuck out early and gotten pizza on the way home. We were fancy like that.

"What are you going to do to celebrate your promotion?" Henrietta asked.

"Henry and I are going away to New York City for the weekend," I told her. "We figured we'd take advantage of the long weekend for Memorial Day."

"That sounds fun. I can check on Marvin while you're gone, if you'd like."

After we'd gotten engaged for real, Henry had moved into my house, renting out his place for extra income. My feral cat Marvin still hated him, but he loved Henry's mom, probably because she always brought him fresh tuna.

"Mrs. Mason." A local reporter shoved closer, breaking into our tiny circle.

"That's Ms. McNally," Henry corrected him firmly, completely supportive of my decision to keep my maiden name. My mother had been horrified, of course, but Dad had shared with me privately that he liked the idea.

"It wouldn't be the Seagulls without a McNally at the helm," he'd told me.

"Ms. McNally," the reporter corrected himself. "You're a woman in a man's sport. What do you attribute your success to?"

"Hard work. A little luck. And an appreciation of what's important in life," I answered, squeezing Henry's hand. "Now if you'll excuse me, my husband and I have something important that we have to attend to."

The reporter scurried off and Henry whispered in my ear, "You want me to lick your flower, don't you?"

"Of course."

***

Hey there! If you liked this book, please show me some love, and leave a review. Good reviews are like puppies, they make everyone feel happy.

Want more midlife romance? Check out the entire Boozy Book Club series to read about how Anges, Evie, and all the other book club members found love later in life. Binge the whole series now at books2read.com/rl/boozybooks[1].

Keep reading for a special excerpt from "Summer Wedding[2]," available now.

Special Preview

Summer Wedding by Rose Bak

"Uncle Reed, when will you get here?"

I smiled at Jonathon's eager tone, even though he couldn't exactly see me through the car dashboard.

"I'm pulling into the parking lot now," I told him as I swung into an open parking spot that came up unexpectedly. "I'll...oh shit!"

"What's the matter?"

"I need to go, I'll call you when I'm checked in."

I clenched the steering wheel and took a deep breath, raising my head to look at the woman who was now on the hood of my car. The very angry woman. Our eyes met through the windshield and for a moment I lost my breath. She was beautiful.

Mentally shaking myself, I turned off the car and got out. My heart was racing. I couldn't believe I'd almost hit someone. I hadn't even seen her.

"I am so sorry. Are you okay? Do you need medical attention?"

The woman made to roll off the hood of the car and I rushed over to help her. I took her hand and everything inside me stilled. *Mine.* The word reverberated through my skull as what felt like an electrical current traveled between our palms.

"Careful," I said softly, my voice rough.

The woman stood up, brushing off her clothing. She was about my age, late forties or early fifties, with a trim, athletic figure. Faded jeans lovingly hugged her slim legs and narrow waist, and her tank top showed toned arms and generous breasts that I was itching to get my hands on. She had thick brown hair that fell past her shoulders in a cascade. Her eyes were chestnut brown, huge in her pale white face, and she had the cutest little button nose. And then there was her mouth...pouty thick lips, slick with some kind of gloss, and pressed together in a frown that told me she wasn't happy.

Oh yeah, probably because I'd hit her with my car.

"Are you okay?" I asked again. "I'm not sure what happened."

Her eyes narrowed in a glare.

"You were driving too fast and too busy talking on your phone to notice I was crossing through this parking space," she told me. "I jumped up on the hood to avoid being crushed."

She pointed at the car in the spot in front of me. There was maybe six inches between the bumper of that car and mine. Jesus. If she hadn't jumped up I might have crushed her. Whoever this woman was, she had good reflexes. I felt sick to my stomach at the idea that I could have seriously hurt her by not paying attention.

"Are you injured?" I asked.

She looked thoughtful and I had the sense she was doing a scan of her body for injuries.

"Probably bruised but nothing's broken, thank God."

"Let me make this right," I said, giving her a smile that had melted a lot of panties in my forty-nine years on this Earth. "Can I buy you dinner later? Or maybe a drink after you check in?"

Her spine snapped straighter, and she gave me a glare that could melt steel.

"Are you seriously hitting on me after you damn near ran me over?"

"Oh. Ah. No," I lied. "I just...what can I do to make it up to you?"

"Watch where you're going next time," she growled. "The next person you try to run over might not be as lucky."

She bent over to pick up the suitcase that she must've dropped when she was evading my car, and I absolutely did not check out her heart-shaped ass. Without another word, she started to walk away at a fast clip.

"At least let me give you my phone number," I said, jogging to catch up with her. "You can call me if you need anything."

She picked up her pace. "Leave me alone, asshole!"

Raising the middle finger of one hand over her shoulder to let me know what she thought of me, she stormed off towards the Main Lodge.

I sat back down in my car, feeling shaken. I couldn't decide if it was because of the near-miss of hitting the woman, or if it was my response to the woman herself. Even angry and flipping me off, there was something about her that called to me. I'd never felt this way about anyone before.

And you let her get away, dumbass, I told myself.

I gathered up my suitcase and headed into the lodge to check in, my pulse still racing. The woman was clearly staying here, so I'd just have to keep a look out for her. If we were meant to be – and I had no doubt that we were – fate would bring her to me again sooner or later.

***

For more of Reed and Erika's story check out Summer Wedding, available at select online retailers. For more information visit my website at bit.ly/AuthorRoseBak[1].

---

1. *https://books2read.com/ap/RDOk1w/Rose-Bak*

Other Books by Rose Bak

Boozy Book Club Series
Beach Reads
Bubbly & Billionaires
Martinis & Mysteries
Bourbon & Bikers
Midlife Madness
Extra Innings
The Proposal Solution

The Good with Numbers Holiday Romance Series
Love Unmasked
The Thanksgiving Scrooge
Maid for Christmas
Countdown to Love
Valentine's Lottery
Christmas Angel

Loving the Holidays Contemporary Romance Series
Dating Santa
New Year's Steve
Independence Dave
Comfort & Joy
Faking It with the Detective
Dropping the Ball
Island Getaway

Midlife Crisis Contemporary Romance Series
Summer Wedding
Roasting with Rob
Christmas Punch
Disaster Planning
Second Chance to Score
Factory Reset

Saving Texas
Texas Christmas
Canadian Doctor
Romancing the Storm
The Oliver Boys Band Contemporary Romance Series
Until You Came Along
Rock Star Teacher
Rock Star Writer
Rock Star Neighbor
Rock Star Lawyer
Silver Fox Falls Midlife Romance
Unexpected Gift
Magical Midlife Series
Beltane Magic (prequel)
Love Potion
Psychic Flashes
Halloween Surprise
Giant Love
Kitchen Magic
Bite-Sized Shifters Paranormal Romance Series
Long Distance Wolf
Wolf Doctor
Kat's Dog
Designer Wolf
Wolf Sheriff
Cocktail Wolf
Second Chance Wolf
Runaway Wolf
Holidays with the Shifters Series
Santa's Claws
Bear Humbug
Jingle Bear

Silver Paws

Joy to the Wolf

Lion's Heart

The Diamond Bay Contemporary Romance Series

Brand New Penny

Fresh as a Daisy

Right as Rain

Reunited Series

Together Again

Finding My Baby

King of the Reunion

Caught by My Best Friend

Standalones

Beach Wedding

Jessie's Girl

Non-fiction

What to Do If You Find a Cougar in Your Living Room: Self-Care in an Uncaring World

It's All About Relationships: Reflections on Love, Friendship, and Connection

Catch up with these and other stories coming soon. Join my newsletter for more information[1] or follow my author page on your favorite retailer.

---

1.   *https://storyoriginapp.com/giveaways/62ee758e-068f-11eb-904e-c373f6014fe1*

About the Author

Rose Bak has been obsessed with books since she got her first library card at age five. She is a passionate reader with an e-reader bursting with thousands of beloved books.

Although Rose enjoys writing both fiction and nonfiction, romance novels have always been her favorite guilty pleasure, both as a reader and an author. Rose's contemporary romance books focus on strong female characters over thirty-five and the alpha males who love them. Expect a lot of steam, a little bit of snark, and a guaranteed happily ever after.

Rose lives in the Pacific Northwest with her family, and special needs dogs. In addition to writing, she also teaches accessible yoga and loves music. Sadly, she has absolutely no musical talent, so she mostly sings in the shower.

Please sign up for the Rose Bak Romance newsletter[1] to get a free book and keep up to date on all the latest news. You can also follow Rose on Facebook[2], Instagram[3], Twitter[4], Goodreads[5], or Bookbub[6].

---

1. https://storyoriginapp.com/giveaways/62ee758e-068f-11eb-904e-c373f6014fe1

2. https://www.facebook.com/AuthorRoseBak

3. https://www.instagram.com/authorrosebak/

4. https://twitter.com/AuthorRoseBak

5. https://www.goodreads.com/authorrosebak

6. https://www.bookbub.com/authors/rose-bak

Don't miss out!

Visit the website below and you can sign up to receive emails whenever Rose Bak publishes a new book. There's no charge and no obligation.

https://books2read.com/r/B-A-VATM-HFDTC

BOOKS 2 READ

Connecting independent readers to independent writers.